TRIBULATION

BOOK DESCRIPTION

Forced off Earth because of an alien invasion, our haggard crew must find a new home. While Infinity One is designed for deep space flight, it is virtually untested as it sets out on its maiden voyage into the solar system.

Running from the aliens and plagued by disasters, the gang retreats to the moon and Proxima b. However, fate has a mind of her own when they end up back on Mars. The fifth seal opens full force when they meet up once again with ol' Randolph Watson.

A crew member turns on the others. Jack is stranded and alone. And Sarah takes on a new and unexpected role.

Follow the exhausted team and find out who must be sacrificed to appease the gods.

ConnieMyres.com

TRIBULATION

Seven Seals Redux, #5

Connie Myres

ConnieMyres.com
FEATHER AND FERMION PUBLISHING

Feather and Fermion Publishing

DEDICATION

To my family, my friends, and those who have supported me though my journey as an author. I appreciate you.

CONTENTS

ONE

Rev. 6:9-11. 9 When he opened the fifth seal, I saw under the altar the souls of those who had been slain for the word of God and for the witness they had borne; 10 they cried out with a loud voice, "O Sovereign Lord, holy and true, how long before thou wilt judge and avenge our blood on those who dwell upon the earth?" 11 Then they were each given a white robe and told to rest a little longer, until the number of their fellow servants and their brethren should be complete, who were to be killed as they themselves had been.

* * *

"I have us in orbit, and the cloaking device is activated," astronaut Ray Barber said as he leaned back in the captain's seat of Infinity One, the new deep-space vessel developed by the Intercosmic Space Program (ISP).

Professor Jerry Dillon, sitting to the right of Ray at the control table, looked out the forward window. There before them was Earth. Not a planet with blue ocean water, hazel continents, and swirling white clouds, but rather a world painted with a blush of pink, adorned with near imperceptible red glitter. "I'd say the view of Earth was beautiful if it were not for the destruction caused by that alien moss. It's an unpleasant reminder that we cannot go back there."

"I'm with you on that," Max said, leaning forward to get a better view of the monitors. He adjusted the thick glasses resting on his nose and then looked at Ray sitting next to him. "If I'm reading this correctly, it says the whole planet is covered with that stuff. Even the oceans and the poles are being . . . digested by that crap."

Ray looked at the screen where the scientist was pointing. "I think you're right."

"You don't know?" Jack said, leaving his seat at the back of the circular main level of the craft. He took off the green coveralls he had taken from the alien base on Mars and walked up behind the three men still sitting at the control desk. "I thought you were an expert in all this space stuff, Ray."

Ray swiveled his chair to look at Jack. "I know Pegasus and the space station inside and out, but Infinity One . . . well, it's new and I'm just one of the test pilots, not one of the people who designed it."

"Can you do more than orbit this spaceship?" Jack said, admiring the surreal view out the window. Larger than a picture window in a house, it took up most of the flight deck's curved wall on the other side of the navigation console.

"It might take a little trial and error to maneuver Infinity One, but don't you worry," Rays said, turning back toward the monitors. "I'm sure they had time to get the fail-proof mechanisms working."

"What?" Jack said, placing his hands on his hips. "You mean we're riding in a half-baked ship?"

Ray laughed. "Something like that. But I assume most things are in place."

"What fail-proof systems are not in place?" Professor Dillon asked, raising an eyebrow.

Ray shrugged. "I'm not sure. I guess we'll find out when the time comes."

Jack crossed his arms, flexing the muscles underneath the tattoo of a colorful Phoenix that extended past the sleeve of his T-shirt. "Do you mean to say that you have us up here in orbit, where we can die from lack of oxygen or burn up in the atmosphere because you don't know how to drive this contraption?"

"Relax," Ray said. "Take a gander at the planet. Would you rather be down there or up here?"

Jack shook his head. "I see your point. I guess we're better off up here."

While the kids, two dogs, and Father Mitch walked around the flight deck—paying particular attention to the seven-foot-tall robot standing in the center of the room—Sarah, Clare, and Tony joined the others on the bridge.

Sarah stood next to Jack. "I suppose we're homeless now."

"Looks like it," Jack said, moving closer to Sarah until his arm touched hers. "Since Earth is out of the picture, at least until that . . . monster moss . . . finishes doing what it's doing. So, where do we go from here?"

"Definitely not back to Earth," Max said, rubbing the coarse whiskers on his face. "That moss is half plant and half animal, so until it finishes its job of changing the earth to something the aliens want, I suggest we get this figured out before the invaders come back from wherever they are."

"Let's consider our options," the professor said, twisting his chair, and his hefty body, to face the adults standing around him. "We could stay in orbit and hope the cloaking shield stays up, or we could go to one of the planets, or one of their moons, and set down until we decide what to do."

"The aliens are going to return, and I don't want to be anywhere near them," Max said. He unzipped the front of the green Mars worker overalls he was wearing, exposing the picture of a skull on the T-shirt beneath. He pulled out the hem of the black cotton fabric and wiped his glasses. "Besides, I have the feeling their spaceship is more high-tech than ours; they'll probably be able to find us."

"Why don't you take those damned work clothes off, Max?" Jack said. "I hate being reminded of that base . . . and Randy."

Max placed the glasses back on his face and looked down at his clothes. Underneath the one-piece garment was black goth attire. "I would, but you jackasses brought me back clothes that make me look ridiculous. I'm a middle-aged man, not a teenager."

Suddenly, an alarm on the console began sounding.

"What's that?" the professor asked, looking at the flashing red light.

"I presume it means the aliens are approaching," Ray said, looking at what appeared to be a radar screen, showing an incoming object.

"The dark side of the moon," Tony blurted out. "We can hide there."

"Good idea," Ray said, placing one hand on the control column and another over a touch display. Then he guided Infinity One to the moon, circling around to the far side, the side that is never seen from Earth, and hopefully not seen by the aliens.

TWO

"Hold on," Ray shouted as he lowered the ship toward the rugged terrain and the many impact craters that marred the surface. "This might be a rough landing."

"Hold on?" Jack said, as he and the others ran back to the flight seats and buckled up. "I thought this thing only had smooth rides."

"It does," Ray said, frantically handling the controls. "But landing it is not my forte, especially when there aren't many flat areas on this side of the moon."

"There's a flat mare over there," the professor said, pointing to the screen. "It should be okay to land on."

Infinity One wobbled and spun in slow motion as Ray lowered it onto the rim of a basaltic lava flow from an ancient volcano. The craft skidded and stopped.

"That wasn't so bad," Ray said, with a tone of self-congratulation.

"What are you talking about?" Max scoffed. "I'm surprised I'm not heaving my guts out from all that spinning. I think you need to take some landing lessons."

"It could've been worse," Ray said, still tending to the lights on the screen until most of the blinking had stopped.

"So where have you actually driven this thing before?" Max asked. He watched Ray's every move, like an apprentice being trained to relieve the captain.

"Only in orbit around Earth. But I'd say you're pretty lucky getting to hang around me." Ray smiled and looked at Max. "Otherwise, that man-eating moss would be stripping the meat from your bones; whatever meat you have on that scrawny body of yours."

"Wow," Willis said, setting the little teacup poodle—Miss Foo—onto the floor next to Jibber. "We're actually on the moon."

Past the forward window lay a barren, yet beautiful landscape. Infinity One was sitting inside a massive crater, on an elevated portion of the two-mile-high rim. Across the nearly one hundred seventy-five-mile-wide basin lay a vast open area, partially covered in shadow. It was as though they were sitting on the edge of a bottomless black hole.

"It has an orange tint," Sarah said, finally loosening the tight grip she had on the seat. "I always considered the moon to be a gray color."

"It's the color of cheese," Georgie said, walking toward the window with Jibber at his side.

"It looks like we've landed on one of the higher points inside the Moscoviense basin," the professor said. "But I wouldn't go walking around out there because the floor of the crater is three or four miles down. We're in a rather precarious position, but at least we're hidden."

"What about the light?" Jack had a confused look on his face as he walked with Sarah back to the control area. "I thought the moon was dark on this side."

"Many people don't realize this, but both sides of the moon get the same amount of sunlight; they are opposite each other. The far side of the moon is not the dark side of the moon," the professor said, running a hand through his disheveled gray hair. "When the near side is fully lit at full moon, then the far side is dark. And when the side we see is dark and in the new moon phase, lit only by Earthshine, then the back side is fully lit."

"I hate to cut your science lesson short, Professor, but we need to do a weapons check while we have a chance," Clare said. She put a hand on her empty holster. "My forty-four Magnum was taken and is someplace inside the Mars station . . . so I'm weaponless. I see Ray still has the M16. How about you guys?"

"I've got nothin," Tony said. "Is there anyone who actually has something, besides Ray?"

"I've got Rausuca's alien wand," Sarah said. She unzipped the cross-body purse—that rarely left her body—and took it out.

"Hey," Ray said in a tone that was so loud and stern that it startled her. "Be careful with that thing."

Sarah put it back into her purse as Jack took the alien pistol from the back waistband of his blue jeans. "I still have this beauty."

Everyone else muttered to the contrary. Their guns, Georgie's sword, and even Father's rosary were on the list of items taken.

"Still got mine. I don't think most of the people in The Community even knew I had it." Professor Dillon patted the pistol in his hip holster that was hidden under his long vest. Then he took a pill bottle from an inside vest pocket. "I even have my blood pressure pills, but they're not going to last forever."

"We have no more ammunition, other than what's on us right now, so the only weapons that are worth anything are the alien pistol and Sarah's magic wand," Clare said, adjusting the camouflage cap that sat snuggly over her overgrown brown bob haircut.

"Does this ship have any weapons?" Tony asked as he walked up to Ray who was powering down Infinity One and settling in for what could be a long haul.

"Yeah, it does," Ray said. "Other than the cloaking shield, it has a laser-type gun, but I don't think it's been tested much."

"I'm hungry," Georgie said, petting Jibber's head. "Is there any food onboard?"

With the M16 still slung over his shoulder, Ray said, "As soon as I figure out what the aliens are doing, I'll give everyone the grand tour."

"I was hoping you weren't going to leave the flight deck, quite yet, with the aliens so close by," Max said, looking at a screen with a relatively sharp image of the unearthly craft orbiting Earth. "I'm actually quite surprised this is able to pick up their spaceship, especially since we're shielded from radio waves."

"Infinity One uses an advanced laser-based system," Ray said. "I don't know much about it, but it appears to be detecting the bad guys quite well."

"Can they detect us?" the professor asked, taking an overused handkerchief from a pocket to wipe his nose.

"As long as we have the cloaking device activated, we should be invisible." Ray pointed at a display panel. "This shows that the shield is at one-hundred percent. We're fine."

Everyone looked out the windows, awestruck by the ragged outline of the mountainous rim from the impact craters around them. Giant stair-like terraces—one of which they had sat down on—lined a portion of the interior walls of the Sea of Moscow.

"What now?" Jack asked, rubbing the tension from the back of his neck.

"I suppose we wait until those extraterrestrials leave and then we can go someplace safer," Ray said. He nodded toward the window. "I don't want our craft to slip off the ledge and into that hole."

"Safer?" Max said, clearing his throat. "Where is that? The only place we can actually leave this ship is the land inside Mars. Unfortunately, that place has half-breeds and their human workers who want us dead, not to mention the dinosaurs."

Ray stood up and stretched. "Infinity One does have an experimental propulsion system that is able to travel faster than the speed of light. If worse comes to worse, we could try it out and go to another star system like Alpha Centauri. It's the closest one to us, and there might be an inhabitable planet for us to live on."

"That's impossible," Max said, leaning back in the copilot's seat. "Nothing can go faster than the speed of light. And even if this thing could travel at one-hundred-eighty-six-thousand miles per second, it would take a few years to even get there. During that time, we could run into problems. Like what if the engine malfunctions and reverts to the speed of the old space shuttle? If that were to happen, it would take thousands of years to get there. We'd all be decayed skeletons by the time we reached our destination."

"So what type of propulsion system does Infinity One have?" the professor asked, nodding in agreement to Max's statement. As an astrophysicist, the professor was not only interested in identifying and studying near earth objects at the observatory with Max but also had an interest in interstellar medium and concepts such as an event horizon. The topic was an entertaining area of study for him, rather than an area of focus in the class he taught at Western. "Nuclear fission or antimatter?"

"Like I said, I'm only the test pilot." Ray watched the professor swallow one of the blood pressure pills without water. "But it also has the ability to use wormholes."

"Like on the television program, *Farscape*?" Sarah said, intrigued. "You mean we'll be going through tunnels in space?"

"That's what they told me," Ray said, taking in a deep breath.

"Let me guess," Max said, looking over the rims of his glasses. "You don't know how to use it."

"I have a good idea how it works," Ray said, ignoring Max's grumpiness. After everything they had been through together, there was no sense taking the cranky scientist's remarks personally. "We just need to know where we're going."

"I didn't realize we were so far along with traversable wormholes," the professor said. "However, I am aware that the mathematics have been extensively studied."

Tony looked back at Dawn, cradling the teacup poodle in her arms. Then he put an arm around Clare's waist. Even though he, Clare, and his father-in-law, Professor Dillon, were trained survivalist, he had no experience in this type of catastrophic event. "Well, I say, that if the aliens figure out where we're at and they start firing on us, I suggest you hit the warp drive button and get us the hell out of here."

"Don't worry; I don't plan on dying today," Ray said. Then he looked at Max who was staring at him with a look of dread. "Do you mind manning the helm? I'm going to show everyone around the ship."

Max's eyes quickly opened and closed behind the thick lenses of his glasses. Then he turned his gaze to the image of the alien craft still orbiting Earth. "Just be sure to point me to the head when you get back."

"Does the robot talk?" Georgie asked. He pointed to the human-like machine that was taller than everyone else and was standing motionless in the center of the flight deck. Looking like a GI Joe soldier doll that the fairy tale giant Blunderbore would have played with as a young ogre, its appearance was rather intimidating. Dressed in military fatigues and combat boots, it was evident the humanoid was meant to be deadly.

"That's Artie," Ray said, cheerfully walking up to it. "He's an android."

"Does it work?" Sarah asked, stroking her hair as she stood away from it.

"Of course he does." Ray motioned for Sarah to stand next to him. "I'll introduce you to him."

"It's not going to kill me, is it?" Sarah said, as she hesitantly walked to Ray's side. "It looks pretty strong."

"First of all, it's not an it, it's a he," Ray said as if the robot were an actual human. "And no, he won't harm a hair on your pretty little head. Artie's AI is programmed to protect us. Not only does he resemble a human—well, somewhat—he acts like a human. I'll wake him up for you."

Ray held up his hand with the palm facing the robot, the same way he opened the airlock door to Infinity One. "Wake up, Artie."

The android blinked and his extremities twitched for only a moment. With a voice that sounded like that of HAL 9000 from the movie 2001: A Space Odyssey, it said, "Hello, Ray Barber. Nice to see you again."

Father Mitch walked around Artie, studying the android and its stiff posture before standing next to Sarah. "Did you do that with that chip in your hand, Ray?"

"Yeah. It's a rather useful device. I don't need to remember passwords or keep track of keys," Ray said, grinning as he touched the palm of his hand.

Wrinkling his brow, Father asked, "Are those of us without implants able to control him?"

Ray gave Father a darting gaze. "If I tell him to accept you as a companion, he will listen."

"What happens if you don't say we're companions?" Father asked, suspiciously eyeing Ray's body language. "What does he do then?"

"Artie will ignore orders from you, other than simple requests, like telling him to move the hell out of your way." Ray bounced up on his toes, apparently amused with his remark.

"Is he a weapon?" Tony asked. He blew out a loud breath as he walked around the android, looking for signs of anything that could cause bodily injury. Artie was bigger than any of them and probably capable of killing a human, or alien for that matter, with its bare hands.

Ray watched Tony scrutinize Artie, then he forced an unnatural laugh.

Max shouted from across the room. "Let me guess, you don't know much about his artificial intelligence, either."

Ray huffed as he glared at Max who was still focused on the monitors. Then he regained a calm composure. "If you must have more details, I'm told he is also programmed to protect the human race by any means necessary."

"By any means necessary?" Tony said, now standing on the other side of the android. "You might as well come clean, Ray. It's not like there's anyone left to throw you in the clink for exposing top secret projects."

Jack laughed. "Isn't that the truth? There's no Clink, Leavenworth, or prison of any sort to worry about anymore. But I'm not sure if that's good or bad because whatever humans are left, can now make up their own rules. We could be living in a Mad Max universe."

"Not entirely," Tony said, raising his voice. "The president, along with the top brass, and other members of the New World Order are probably in a bunker inside Cheyenne Mountain while—we the people—-are left to fend for ourselves. That complex sits under thousands of feet of granite and can survive earthquakes, EMPs and any nuclear attack known to man."

"It's totally unfair that they get protected only because of their status, but at least we made it onto Infinity One," Clare said. She looked at Ray who was looking back at her in agreement. "Are there any more ships like this one?"

Ray nodded. "The Intercosmic Space Program was working on a sister ship called Morning Glory. I didn't test pilot that ship so I don't know much about it. However, I think ISP had facilities in other countries, too, but I have no idea how far along they were in development and testing."

"So they were already aware that this was coming?" Sarah said, still standing next to Ray. She smelled the bold maverick scent of his deodorant, radiating from his warm body, as he unzipped the front of his orange NASA flight suit. Sarah looked at him, and he looked back at her with a smile as he pulled his arms out from the sleeves and then secured the fabric at his waist, revealing a gray perspiration-stained T-shirt. Sarah felt embarrassed for staring at his toned chest muscles, so she forced her eyes back to his. "Does that mean there is a possibility that there are other people out there just like us?"

"I don't have any idea," Ray said, facing Sarah. He put his thumbs in the material tied at his waist as if he were a cowboy, relaxed and confident. "But if they did, this . . . dystopia, happened before they had time to work out all the kinks."

Jack knew he was not the sharpest tool in the shed, but he could tell when a man was coming on to a woman and he believed Ray wanted a relationship with Sarah, and she was taking the bait. Sure, Sarah was an adult, and she could be with anyone she wanted if she wanted anyone at all, but he did not entirely trust Ray. But he also knew that he himself had feelings for Sarah. Even though they had not slept together, he did not want Ray seducing her, making her do something against her better judgment. Jack cracked his knuckles, momentarily catching Ray's attention and the smirk Ray shot toward him.

"Let's get this show on the road," Professor Dillon said as he walked to the back of the room. He sat down in one of the protective launch seats where he was able to elevate his edematous ankles. "I'm about ready for a nap."

Ray looked at the android, standing at attention, waiting for instructions. "Artie, I'd like you to meet my friend, Sarah. Would you please welcome her aboard Infinity One?"

The humanoid looked at Sarah and smiled. Its eyes blinked, and its pale red lips formed a charming grin. If it were not for the fact that she was aware that it was a robot, she might have mistaken him for a living male—perhaps a tall basketball player—under different circumstances. "I am pleased to meet you, Sarah. Welcome aboard Infinity One, the first intergalactic spacecraft known to mankind."

"It's nice to meet you, too, Artie." Sarah felt odd speaking to something made of synthetic material, but she would go along with the high-tech demonstration.

Everyone, including Sarah, backed away from the platform when Artie stepped off the pedestal he was standing on, took a few steps, and then stood in front of Sarah and Ray. He held out his hand, in greeting, to Sarah.

Sarah shook Artie's hand. "His skin feels so . . . real, and his grip is so gentle."

"Do not be afraid of me," Artie said, releasing Sarah's hand. "I am here to help you. I am programmed with the latest learning software, able to perceive the environment and take appropriate actions based on human intelligence and machine learning. My actions and emotions are ethical and logical, avoiding the common flaws of human behavior."

"He's like a bodyguard," Willis said, his eyes wide with amazement.

Artie turned and looked at Willis. "That is correct, Willis."

"You know my name?" Willis glanced at both Georgie and Dawn before nodding enthusiastically at Artie's skills of perception.

"I've been observing everyone inside Infinity One," Artie said, then he looked at Ray. "No threats have been detected."

"No threats? What do you call this alien spaceship?" Max said, pointing at the monitor.

"I believe Artie is talking about us," Clare said, looking over her shoulder at Max. "He doesn't perceive us as threats."

"And what if he did?" Jack said, directing his question to Ray. "Would you be able to stop him from doing something that he shouldn't be doing?"

Ray grinned. "Don't worry, Jack, Artie isn't stupid. I think everyone is overreacting. I realize it's your first time seeing an android, but imagine Artie as your big brother. And even if any one of us were to do something that may be mistaken for a threat, he is intelligent enough to know that it's only you behaving like a jackass."

Jack was not sure if Ray was directing the comment about acting like a jackass directly to him, or in general. Even though he had not known Ray for very long, he liked him, for the most part. Especially since he was the one who piloted the Pegasus capsule off the aliens' bioship and took them to safety. But now they were in Ray's territory onboard his futuristic spaceship with an eerily human-looking cyborg soldier. Of course, Jack was aware he could be overreacting because of Ray's apparent—or imagined—interest in Sarah. Not to mention the weirdness of that damned chip in Ray's hand. "I just don't want him to vaporize any of us."

Ray laughed. "You'll get used to Artie. He might even save your life someday."

Suddenly an alarm began to sound, like that of a pinging fire alarm.

"What's that?" Sarah said. Amber caution lights caught her attention as she watched Ray dart back to the control desk.

"The cloaking shield is malfunctioning, Ray," Artie said as he stepped back onto the pedestal. "I will try to repair it."

"Crap!" Max shouted. "The alien spaceship is moving, and I think it's headed our way."

THREE

Jack and Tony ran up behind Max and Ray to see what was going on while the women instructed the kids to get back into the flight chairs.

"Artie," Ray said as he frantically pressed buttons. "Are you able to get the shield back up before the aliens find us?"

"I am working on it, Ray," Artie said, unruffled by the commotion.

"The aliens must know we're here because they began moving when the shield malfunctioned," Max said, wiping his moist palms onto his pant legs.

Jack watched as Ray enlarged the screen that showed the Infinity One blanketed with a flickering fog. "Is that the force field?"

"It's the cloaking shield, Jack," Ray said, perturbed. "We don't have enough energy for both."

Jack was not sure whether to be relieved that the ship actually had a protective barrier, or whether to strap himself into a seat next to the kids because they were unable to use it.

"You've got to be kidding," Max said, pointing to the image he had been observing for the last hour. "But it looks like those damned aliens are almost above us."

Ray worked swiftly as he scanned the monitors and manipulated controls. "Artie, whatcha got for us?"

"The cloaking device is at fifty percent. That is the best I can do until Infinity One has time to recharge the plasma particles. We had launched before it was fully operational," Artie said, as calmly as a mother trying not to panic her children. "They can sense our presence but cannot pinpoint our location. If the shield fails further, I will employ the force field."

"Thank you, Artie," Ray said, finally resting his hands on the desktop.

Jack was afraid to speak or move, unsure if any activity or sounds would be detected by the enemy above them. He did not want to end up inside the bioship's stomach again or jailed in one of those black boxes.

Ray silenced the alarms, making the flight deck as quiet as a classroom during an exam. Even the dogs made no noise, aside from an occasional click of a dog's nails on the floor and the breathy sound of panting, no one moved.

With the side of his hand, Jack wiped a bead of sweat from the stubble on his upper lip as he continued staring at the image with the cloaking device prominently displayed. Many numbers, equations, and words flashed on the screen, but the one that read fifty percent had to be the shield's strength. Unfortunately, the digits were jumping around. One moment it read fifty-one percent and the next, it was down to forty-nine. It was like watching a boiler's pressure gauge punch into the red, hoping it would not explode.

"Looks like the aliens are moving away," Max whispered as he rubbed the gray hairs on his chin. "They're not even going back to Earth orbit where they had been."

"They've given up," Ray said, letting out a sigh of relief. "They probably thought it was an anomaly, but I wouldn't be surprised if they come back."

"Yeah, an anomaly from one of the ancient moon bases," Tony said, crossing his arms.

"There you go again with your conspiracy theories," Max said, leaning back in the copilot's seat.

"It's not a conspiracy theory, it's a fact," Tony said, widening his stance. "I even saw towers and ancient ruins when we were landing; not too far from where we are now."

"It's just some weird lunar artifacts," the professor said, ambling up to them. Despite the extra weight his legs had to carry, he was able to get around without much difficulty. "They only appear to be artificial structures."

"You're wrong again, Professor," Tony said, shaking his head. "NASA and the Navy like to tamper with the images taken by Apollo and other missions. I'd like for the both of us to put on a spacesuit and go look at them. Then you will see for yourself that they are real. Besides, what did you call this place we landed in?"

"It's known as Mare Moscoviense," the professor said, letting the words roll off his tongue as if he were a professor at an Ivy League school rather than a public university.

"For your information, one of the major newspapers reported a triangular object with rows of lights in this area," Tony said, lifting his chin. "And that was mainstream news."

"I remember that," the professor said, stuffing his hands into his vest pockets. "It was caused by a stitching artifact in the photograph, like a mosaic."

"I say we go check it out," Tony said, looking toward the inner equipment airlock as though he was ready to don a suit that very moment.

"Besides, we're in a spaceship on the moon, so why are things like moon bases still so hard for you to believe in?"

The professor cleared his throat. "Because this is now, not thousands of years ago."

"You're fighting a losing battle," Jack said, giving Tony a look of, 'just give it up, pal.' "We've been down this road before."

"I'll go outside with you," Willis said, getting out of the flight seat he was lounging in as if it were an Adirondack chair.

"No one is going anywhere right now." Ray turned the captain's chair to face the others. "If the aliens return and we have to leave the moon quickly, you'll get left behind."

"The dogs have to pee," Dawn said, watching Jibber sniff around Artie's pedestal as if looking for a spot to relieve herself.

Max watched both dogs, with their noses to the floor, search for what they could not find, a perfect patch of grass. "I think you'd better continue that tour, Ray, before one of those mutts stink up the joint."

Ray followed Max's eyes to where the antsy dogs were beginning to whine. "Let's continue our little excursion and take care of the dogs before they can't hold it anymore."

"I don't think I can hold it anymore," Willis said, squeezing his legs together for fun.

Georgie and Dawn laughed as Ray led them to the elevator at the back of the room. Willis and Georgie climbed down the ladder while everyone else, except Max, Jack, and Father who were manning the helm, took the easy way to the deck below.

"This level is the living area. The cabins, galley, sickbay, and lavatory are on this lower deck," Ray said walking off the elevator. "There is an area in the greenhouse where the dogs can do their business; that'll be our first stop."

"Wow, there's so much room down here." Sarah was amazed at how the designers had managed to take a small space and make it feel like an expansive resort.

"Does this vessel utilize augmented reality?" The professor studied the surroundings as if he were in an amusement park's house of mirrors.

Ray nodded as he led the group toward what looked like an opening in the side of the ship. "You impress me, Professor. As I've said before, I'm only a test pilot, but the ship has a way of superimposing computer-generated images into what we see as the real world."

"What keeps us from running into walls?" The professor touched objects—walls, chairs, and anything within reach—as if he was expecting his hand to go right through them.

"If you don't have a chip like I do, you'll need a smart wristband. They're over by the fire extinguishers and the supplemental oxygen."

But it was not until everyone walked into the conservatory that the awesomeness of the spaceship became evident. Underneath a see-through dome, fruit trees, and vegetable plants were thriving. Several paths meandered through the green smelling serene landscape.

"Take the dogs over there." Ray pointed toward what looked like a small park.

"I'm surprised you have a place for Jibber and Miss Foo to go," Clare said, watching the kids take the dogs to a mowed lawn framed with colorful flowerbeds and a bench.

Ray shrugged. "Because of the length of time that people would need to be on the ship for intergalactic travel, accommodations were made for animals like cats and dogs. I guess they felt it was necessary, for the mental health of humans, to be around animals."

Clare reached out and held Tony's hand. "This place is so beautiful, but who takes care of it?"

"Artie does," Ray said, watching Tony pull Clare closer to him. "He's great at multitasking. Most things are automated, like making sure plants have the proper amount of light and water. He can pick the fruit while still monitoring the ship's systems. However, for some things, like fixing a malfunctioning shield requires him to get back to Infinity One's central hookup, the pedestal."

The giddy kids and dogs rejoined the group.

"Do we get to pick out our own rooms?" Georgie asked as they walked out of the greenhouse.

"How many rooms are there?" Clare asked.

Ray could tell by Tony and Clare's body language that they were ready for their private cabin. Then he looked at Sarah who was attentively waiting for his answer. He wanted to touch her delicate-looking cheeks and move her long tangled hair away from her neck. Could she read his thoughts, he wondered, as he smiled at her? "There's enough rooms for everyone. As you know, Infinity One was designed for flights that last years, even a lifetime; that's why we have a greenhouse and AR. There are even stasis units on the deck below us. I've never used one, but they're supposed to put people into a suspended animation so that they can survive super long trips."

"I thought this ship had warp drive," Tony said, scratching his temple. "Why are there stasis chambers?"

Ray rubbed the back of his neck, he was getting tired of answering everyone's questions. "I don't know. But I guess they may have them for backup, just in case there's a problem with the warp drive and wormhole technology. Especially since it hasn't even been tested out in the wild yet."

He continued showing everyone around, beginning with the public restroom. Then he moved on to the cabins where there were two basic sizes; small ones for individuals and larger ones to accommodate two people. Each had at least one bed, an entertainment center, and a private bath.

Ray explained how the kitchen and dining areas were shared and meant to bring people together to avoid isolation. The recreation room had a pool table, computers for gaming, and an attached gym with a treadmill and weights. He finished with the virtual reality room, whereupon entering, the user could select from a variety of artificial environments. Relaxing choices such as a forest with birds and crickets, or more invigorating surroundings such as being immersed in a game with zombies that need to be taken out. The choices were many and meant to prevent cabin fever or to be used for training. "At least that's what they said during orientation."

"Cool, a holodeck," Willis said, looking into the darkened room.

"I hope we don't lose gravity or else those rock hard billiard balls will begin floating around," Tony said as he looked at the pool table that was secured to the floor. Then he looked at Ray who was standing disinterested and appeared ready to leave. "Do we get to go to the level below us?"

Ray's jaw tightened as he led them out of the rec area and back into the central court. "There's no need to go down there at the moment, but I'll show you later. Right now I want to get back to the bridge. You guys can choose your cabins in the meantime."

"Where's your room?" Sarah asked, watching the kids run to the cabins that were far away from the main entrance, yet next to the games.

"I don't have one. But the captain's quarters is over there, so I suppose I'll take that one . . . since I'm now the captain of this frigate." Ray pointed to the room that was obviously meant for a high-ranking crew member. Not only did the steel door look heavily reinforced with bolts, but its number, directly above the entrance was the number one. The rest of the cabins were numbered in sequence around the deck.

As Ray walked to the elevator at a brisk pace, Clare noticed that her father's face was flushed. "Dad, why don't you pick out a room and lie-down for a while. I think your blood pressure is creeping up. Tony and I will take the room next to yours."

The professor looked back at the three noisy kids and the dogs who were laughing and running about as if they were six-year-olds on a playground at recess. "If they're back there, I want a room far away from the ruckus. That one there looks okay, number four."

"The loving grandfather, as always," Clare teased as she nudged her father with an elbow. "We'll take the one to the left of yours, if it doesn't have a tiny bed, that is."

"I guess I'll be your neighbor to the right, I don't want to be too far away from everyone," Sarah said, walking to the number five room.

The automatic door slid open, and Sarah stepped inside. She was surprised at how nice the room was, especially with its muted earth tones of green, brown, and warm grays. There was a single bed with what appeared to be a pull-down bunk bed above it. Artificial plants, a recliner, and a desk with a chair were straightforward and clean. And even though the entertainment center had a computer monitor that took up most of the back wall—next to the door leading into the bathroom—it was unobtrusive. The cabin was nicer than any hotel she had ever been in, even her own home. She had to be dreaming.

First on her mind, though, was using the bathroom. When finished, Sarah looked at her reflection in the mirror. She cringed when she saw her messed up hair, a smudge of something on her cheek, and clothes that looked exactly like what they were—dirty and wrinkled from having not been changed or cleaned in quite some time. But Sarah was too tired to worry about her appearance, so she walked out of the bathroom. Through her open cabin door, she saw the kids chitchatting around three rooms across the way. Then Sarah looked at the bed, the inviting bed. Before going over and seeing what rooms the kids had chosen, she would take a nap and then later she would concern herself with everything else. Right now, at least in relative terms, everyone was safe.

Sarah took the pillow out from under a silver blanket. The fabric was deceptively soft and warm; she expected it to feel like tinfoil. Without even bothering to take off her crossbody purse, she plopped her tired body on the bed and closed her eyes.

Sleep came on fast as the blackness turned to images of her deceased parents. She was a teenager, and they were on a family vacation at the cabin nestled in the Ogemaw Hills. Her dad was building a fire outside so that they could roast hot dogs and marshmallows while her mom was in the family-built A-frame gathering the mustard, ketchup, and buns. Then things began to shake. The bottles fell from her mother's hands as she grabbed hold of the doorframe. Her father dropped hold of a piece of split wood as he lost his footing and fell to the sandy ground. She saw herself running to them shouting, "Earthquake," as a car horn blared.

Then the dream world began to blur with the reality of her body being jostled about while an alarm sounded and panicked people shouted. Sarah was startled awake.

FOUR

"It's a moonquake," Max said, clutching the console table.

Out the forward window, boulders the size of trucks broke free from the rim and down the side of the crater until disappearing into the black abyss.

"Shit, one those could fall on top of us," Jack said, grabbing onto the back of Max's chair. "Put up the force field."

Ray looked at Jack who was trying not to lose his balance. "If the force field goes up, then the cloaking shield will come down."

"If you don't put it up, then we'll be dead, and it won't matter anymore," Jack said.

"I think the aliens are gone," Father said, setting where the professor had been seated next to Ray.

Max kept his eyes on the screen. "You're right. I don't see the bastards anywhere."

"Artie, engage the force field," Ray said.

"Force field engaged, Ray."

The ground continued to shake, causing rocks to fall onto the shield and then gain momentum as they dropped into the depths of the crater.

Several minutes passed before the shaking stopped and the rim's destruction ceased. Moondust obscured the view outside, but it was clear that a bad situation had been made worse.

"Is the ship okay?" Jack said, finally letting go of Max's seatback.

"Artie, status report," Ray said.

"Infinity One sustained minor damage to the port quarter before the shield was engaged,"

"Will we need to make repairs?"

"No repairs are needed, Ray. However, when I lower the force field, debris will fall onto the vessel. It will need to be removed."

"That means someone has to go outside," Jack said.

"That cyborg can go out there." Max waved a hand toward Artie still perched on the pedestal.

"I'll send Artie," Ray said. "He can lift the heavy rocks, but someone should go with him."

No one said anything as everyone from the lower deck began filing onto the main level.

"I hope we're not stuck here," Tony said, walking up to the helm.

"Someone has to suit up and go outside with the robot," Max said.

Sarah walked up and stood next to Jack. They gave each other a nervous smile.

Ray watched as Jack leaned toward Sarah. "I think Jack should go outside with Artie."

Jack frowned. "Why not you? You're the one trained in all this."

"I need to man the helm," Ray said. "I'm the only one that knows how to run the ship, and I should be here in case something else happens."

Max looked at Tony who was smelling the underarms of his olive drab T-shirt. "I think commando guy should go outside. He's the next strongest one, after that thing over there."

"I'll go," Tony said.

"You're too big, you won't fit in my suit," Ray said. "My suit's been tested, and Jack's about my size."

Max smacked his hand on the console and looked at Ray. "Do you mean to say there aren't enough spacesuits for all of us?"

Ray glared at Max. "There are enough suits, but my suit is the only one that's been tested and is safe to use."

"The spacesuits in the equipment room look all right," Clare said, looking through the window of the airlock's door.

Ray looked at Tony. "Well, if you want to take the chance of exploding inside the suit, go right ahead. You can go outside with Artie."

"Wait, I'll go," Jack said. "Just show me what to do."

"Why can't Artie go out there by himself?" Sarah said.

"I believe in the buddy system," Ray said. "It's safer when people are paired up."

"But Artie's a robot," Sarah said. "He's not a human being."

"Artie is crucial to our wellbeing," Ray said. "He monitor's the ship's systems and, quite frankly, can respond faster to emergencies than we can."

"So what exactly do you want me to do?" Jack said.

Ray enlarged a screen so that it displayed a three-dimensional image in front of the control desk. It showed boulders suspended above the aft of Infinity One, near the greenhouse. "Even though the ship is designed to withstand significant force, it has not been tested and cleared for deep space flight. When the force field is lowered so that I can engage the cloaking shield, the debris will fall onto the hull and possibly damage it."

"Can't you just pull away from the rim?" Tony said. "Then the rocks will slide off the shield."

"Have you seen his driving?" Max said. "He'd probably head us into the wall of the crater instead of away from it."

"Thanks for your vote of confidence, Max; but the main reason is that the boulders are straining the shield." Ray pointed toward the screen and the affected part of the protective dome. "The strength of the force field is dropping and will likely continue to do so until we remove the stress. The minute I move the ship, without the cloaking device on, we'll probably be noticed by the aliens."

"The aliens aren't around anymore," Max said.

"How do you know?" Ray said. "They could be cloaked."

Max pinched his lips together in frustration, then said, "You're right, but from what you're saying that force field isn't worth a damn. How can it deflect blasts from the aliens if it can't even support some rocks?"

"Damn it, Max, you know the force field and the cloaking shield aren't working right," Ray said. "I'm doing the best I can with what we got."

"It's settled, I'm going out," Jack said. "But how am I going to lift giant rocks?"

"Artie will do the heavy lifting," Ray said. "I need you to make sure nothing happens to him—we need him. You can move the lighter stuff. Things weigh less on the moon."

"That's right," the professor said, walking from the elevator to a flight seat and new resting spot. "The moon's gravity is only seventeen percent the force of Earth's. A hundred-pound rock will weigh a mere seventeen pounds. And Jack—"

"What?"

"Watch how you walk out there. I don't know how the spacesuits are designed, but you could end up flying into the air and over the edge of the basin if you're not careful."

"You've got to be kidding?"

"Don't worry yourself," Ray said. "The suits adjust for that so you can walk near normal."

"How's he getting through the force field to remove the stuff?" Max asked.

"Artie can open a door."

"What happens if I accidentally run into the force field? I'm not going to get disintegrated, am I?"

"If you're on the inside, then nothing will happen. Outside, you can get shocked, but Artie will disable that layer of protection while you're out there just in case you accidentally walk into it."

"So my life will be in that robot's hands. Isn't that wonderful?"

"If everyone is done questioning me, let's get moving." Ray walked to the airlock, opened the door, and stepped inside. He touched a wall panel, triggering more light to fill the chamber and illuminate the suits.

Jack stepped in behind him. "I didn't notice all these spacesuits earlier."

"Why would you?" Ray opened a locker on the left and took out a garment that looked like long johns covered with narrow tubes. Then he pulled down a bench. "I'll help you put this on. Take off your jeans."

"Gettin' a little fresh, aren't you?"

Then Ray held a pad in front of Jack. "You might need this."

"A diaper? I'll pass," Jack said, stripping down to his underwear. He noticed everyone that was watching turn away at this maneuver. "I can't just get into the suit with my clothes on?"

"You could, but you're going to get hot inside the suit. The long underwear is a liquid cooling and ventilation garment. Believe me, you'll need it, or else the inside of your mask will fog over."

When Jack finished putting on the undergarments, he put on the white lower torso assembly, complete with boots, and then squatted and slid into the hard-shelled upper body assembly attached to the locker wall. Ray attached the pieces together, and then Jack stepped forward. "Not bad."

Ray helped Jack put on a thin cap with earphones and microphones. "This is the communications carrier assembly; we call it the Snoopy Cap."

"Nice. But before you lock me up in this thing, how does it work?"

Ray plugged the cap into the suit. "I'll be able to talk to you from Infinity One, and you and Artie will be able to communicate, as well. Your controls are here on the front of the suit, but the only one you might need to use is this one, the volume control. I'll stay in constant communication with you."

After the gloves and helmet had been attached, Jack turned toward the others—who had returned to watch the show—and gave them a thumbs up.

"Be careful out there, Jack," Sarah said.

"Don't worry, I don't plan on doing anything stupid."

"No one plans for it."

For one fleeting second, Jack wondered if he would ever see Sarah's sweet face again. "I'd kiss ya, but I'm kinda packaged up."

"Can you hear me?" Ray said, through the helmet speakers, sounding a little annoyed.

"Loud and clear."

"I hear you as well. I'll keep the mic on so that I'll be able to hear everything you say."

Everyone moved aside as Artie walked into the airlock. With his smooth voice, he said, "Follow my directions, Jack, and you'll be fine."

Jack supposed it was not going to be the first time his life was in the hands of a machine—and Ray. "Sure thing."

FIVE

"Everyone, move away from the airlock door," Ray said.

When the anxious spectators stepped away from the equipment airlock, Ray closed and sealed the door. Sarah and Tony looked through the window. They saw Jack and Artie talking to each other as Ray had their voices audible throughout the deck.

"Does the Mark Four feel satisfactory to work in?" Artie said.

"Mark Four?"

"The spacesuit you are wearing. Are you ready to leave Infinity One?"

"Do I have a choice?"

"You always have a choice, Jack."

"I'm as ready as I'll ever be."

"I am opening the crew airlock, Ray."

"Copy that, Artie."

The door slid open, and Jack followed Artie into the next room. The door closed behind them.

"You don't need a suit?" Jack said, watching Artie's chest rise and fall as if it were breathing.

"I am designed to appear human. And while I do take a little oxygen into my system, I am not dependent on it. Neither will my body suffer the same deleterious effects as yours, Jack. If you were to develop a hole in your suit, your blood would begin to boil. Your body will expand. Mine will not."

"Thanks for the happy thoughts, Artie. I'm totally having second thoughts about this."

"Do not worry, Jack. The exterior of your suit is tough and will withstand most micrometeoroids."

"Most? If I come back alive, it'll be a miracle." Jack looked through the windows of the doors and saw Sarah looking back at him. If there ever was a reason to risk his life, it was for her. Then his attention was turned to the outer door as it opened and a ramp slid out.

"You're clear to leave the ship," Ray said.

"Follow me." Artie began walking down the ramp.

"Wait. No tether? What if I float off or something?"

Ray's voice filled the helmet. "You don't need a tether; it'll only get in your way."

Jack was not so sure about that. He would feel a lot better if he had one. Especially since the rim they were sitting on was not that far from a ledge that dropped off into something deeper, and more sinister, than the Grand Canyon. He stood there marveling at the massive size of the jagged rim. It was both terrifying and glorious.

"You can go now, Jack," Ray said. "The sooner we get this done the sooner I can enable the cloaking shield."

"Ten-four," Jack said, giving a faux salute.

"Lower the extravehicular visor assembly, Jack," Artie said.

Jack lowered the sun visor and followed Artie down the ramp and onto the moon's surface. Was he the first man to walk on the far side of the moon? "One small step for man. One giant leap for mankind."

Jack heard people whooping and hollering in the background.

Then cranky Max came on. "That's already been said, Jack. Can't you come up with something original?"

"Probably not," Jack said, walking as though he was on thin ice. "I'm concentrating on trying not to fly away or fall through some weird crack."

"Just follow Artie," Ray said. "He won't take you to any unsafe ground."

Jack could not shake the uncertainty of putting his life into the hands of an android that was controlled by Ray. When he looked toward the back of Infinity One, it was then that he realized the breadth of the situation. The huge flying saucer had an invisible dome around it that was only made clear when he saw the landslide suspended tens of feet above it. There was no way he and Artie were going to move all those rocks and boulders.

"Hey, Ray," Jack said, walking to where Artie had stopped and turned to face him. "A part of the embankment has fallen on top of the force field. There's no way we can remove it all."

"It might be easier than you think. Give it a try before you give up."

Jack was not giving up; it just plain made no sense to risk his life working on it. He stopped next to Artie and a wavy reflection on the side of the bubble. "Looks like Artie made a door. I'll check it out."

"Please, follow me," Artie said, walking through the static.

Jack followed him, and it was then, now that he was outside the force field's protection, that he noticed it had a transparent oiliness to it, making it visible. But that was not all, he could no longer see the door.

"Artie, where's the damned door?"

"I closed it because it draws energy. I will reopen it when it is time."

The GI Joe climbed easily up the side of the embankment until he was at the top. He looked down at Jack. "I suggest you work on the rocks where you are at. I will remove the debris from on top and the other side."

"Okay, but I still don't see the point. I think we should pull the ship out enough so that the debris slides off the dome. Then when it's fallen off, we can drop the force field and turn on the cloaking device."

"It's the movement, Jack," Ray said. "I already covered this. Any movement will alert the aliens. It's safer this way. Trust me."

Jack picked up on Ray's rising anger. "Yes, captain."

The professor's voice came through the earpiece. "Tell Jack not to take too long because there could be another quake."

"Did you hear that, Jack?" Max said.

"Yeah, I heard the bad news."

Jack looked up and saw Artie hard at work tossing boulders the size of riding lawn mowers away from the spaceship with ease. They had to weigh over a ton. Jack bent over and picked up a basketball sized rock, expecting it to weigh at least fifty pounds. But when he lifted it, it was so light that he fell backward, almost doing a flip. A flip into the crater's pit.

"Are you all right, Jack?" Max said.

Jack lay motionless on the ground, listening for the sound of an air leak or anything else that would lead to his tragic demise. Everything seemed as it should. He slowly got back to his feet. "I'm fine. That rock was lighter than it looked."

Jack and Artie worked for a couple hours, clearing most of the rubble from above the ship.

"The remaining soil on the force field will not harm Infinity One when the barrier is dropped, and the cloaking shield is engaged," Artie said, standing above the ship like a king of the hill.

"Thank you, Artie," Ray said.

"Can we go inside now," Jack said, fully aware he sounded like a child whose mother had booted him outside to play.

"Yes, you may," Ray said.

Jack began climbing back down to where Artie had previously made the door. He looked up and saw Artie standing still. "Are you coming, big guy?"

"I sense vibrations. Another quake—"

Before Artie could finish the sentence, the ground began to shake as before. Jack lost his footing and slid the rest of the way down the hill. The ground shook as he scrambled to where the door had been.

"Open the door, Artie," Jack said, frantically pushing on the filmy barrier.

When he looked up at Artie, he could not believe what he saw. The damned robot had apparently made a door in the top of the dome because it jumped through, leaving Jack outside.

"Artie, let me in," Jack shouted. But the android was already inside the airlock as the ship slid into the basin.

SIX

"Strap in!" Ray cried out as he pulled the safety harness over his body.

Alarms blared and lights flashed as Infinity One slipped off the shelf and began falling into the Moscoviense basin. Chaos reigned as people ran against the tilted floor. Artie found his spot on the pedestal and just before they crashed into the floor of the crater, the ship abruptly stopped with a bounce as if two like poles of a magnet were repelling each other.

Ray silenced the alarms. "Is everyone all right?"

"I need to check on the kids," Sarah said, making her way to the ladder.

"You stay here," Tony said. "I'll check on them."

"I'm going below, too," Sarah said, leading the way.

"What happened?" Father said, looking at the blackness through the forward window.

Ray turned on the exterior lights. They were suspended just above the ancient volcanic bed. "The second quake collapsed the rim causing us to fall, but Infinity One's safety mechanism and Artie kept us from crashing. Kind of like an airbag."

"What about Jack?" Father said.

Ray looked back and saw that Sarah had gone below with Tony. "I don't know."

"I thought that robot was supposed to protect us," Max said. "He hightailed it inside, leaving Jack out there by himself."

"If it weren't for Artie, we'd all be dead," Ray said.

"Artie probably made the ethical decision—even though it's controversial—that the needs of the many outweigh the needs of the few," the professor said.

"Jack could still be alive," Father said. "Can we go back up and find him?"

"The power's low," Ray said. "Artie, how long before we can move Infinity One?"

"I have disengaged the force field. Tremendous energy was used to prevent Infinity One from the inevitable impact. I will set Infinity One onto the basin floor so that power can be restored and we are able to maneuver the ship to rescue Jack."

"How long is that going to take?" Max said.

"I estimate one hour, possibly two," Artie said.

"Are you able to raise the cloaking shield, Artie?" Ray said.

"No. To repower the drives quickly requires everything, except the life support, to be powered down."

Clare got out of her seat and walked up to the control desk. "Can we talk to Jack?"

"We lost communication when the quake began," Ray said.

Max cleared his throat. "At least, as far as I can tell, the aliens still aren't around."

"That's good," Clare said walking to the elevator. She stepped inside. "The elevator isn't working."

"Artie's powering everything to their bare minimums to speed up the charging," Ray said. "Take the ladder."

The lights dimmed as Infinity One powered down into a hibernation mode.

When Clare reached the lower deck, she saw everyone sitting quietly in the living area. "How is everyone?"

"Everyone's fine, babe," Tony said. "What's going on upstairs?"

"We need to sit tight until the ship is able to recharge its battery, or whatever it's called."

"Any sign of Jack?" Sarah said.

"We're going to look for him in an hour or two." Clare sat next to Tony and Dawn in the lounge, then looked at Sarah. "But don't worry yourself, I'm sure he's fine."

Sarah gave a quick nod, but she was not so sure. Jack was so close to the spaceship when it fell, he could have been pulled along with it. No one could survive a fall like that, even with the moon's gravity in their favor.

"I found a deck of cards," Georgie said, sitting down at a small round table. "Anyone want to play?"

The kids, along with Clare, settled around the table as they discussed what card game they were going to play.

"Do you want to join us, Sarah?" Clare said. "There's not much else to do while we wait for the ship to recharge. It'll keep your mind off . . . things."

Sarah shook her head. "Maybe later."

"I'm going back up to the deck," Tony said.

Sarah watched Tony walk to the ladder and then she looked at the group at the table debating on whether to play euchre, rummy, or poker. Rummy won.

Anxiety grew inside her as she worried about Jack's well-being. Was he alive, injured, or—she could not think about the worst-case scenario. She wanted to run up to the flight deck and force Ray to go back for Jack, whether or not the ship was done recharging.

Sarah sighed. She could not sit still. She needed to walk, to pace, to do something. She stood up and walked to the greenhouse. The scent of citrus intermingled with pine, reminding Sarah of Christmas only a couple days away. She looked up, hoping to see the rim of the basin and Jack waving back at her. But all she saw was darkness.

"Want a cup of coffee?"

Sarah turned to see Ray coming toward her with two paper cups. She took one. "Thanks."

"Thought I'd come down and see how everyone was doing," Ray said, standing at her side. He sipped the coffee. "Artie has everything under control."

"I'm fine, just worried about Jack. Have you been able to locate him?"

"Not yet. When Artie gives the go ahead, we'll power things up and then we should be able to find him."

Sarah moved the hot cup of joe to her other hand without taking a drink.

"I'm sure Jack's okay. We should spend this downtime relaxing, especially since we can't do anything else."

"Is Artie able to go out and find Jack?"

Ray motioned for Sarah to follow him and to sit with him on a bench near a rose bush. "Artie can't. He's optimizing the ship during the recharge. He'll be able to help us later."

Sarah sat next to Ray. She was about to sip her coffee when she noticed Ray looking at her. She turned to see a smile break through a face of unshaven whiskers.

"We've been through so much," Ray said. "But there is one thing I've wanted to ask you. I know it's probably none of my business, but I was wondering if you and Jack are in a relationship."

Sarah looked away. There was only one reason he was asking the question. "We're good friends. I really like Jack; he's helped the kids and me. I owe him my life."

Ray shifted his position and turned toward her. "But you're not . . .?"

Sarah studied his face; he was waiting for her answer. She knew Ray liked her and that he was trying to see where he stood in her eyes. She might as well come out and say it, or else he'll keep asking about it. "If you're asking if we've slept together, the answer is no."

Ray's smile grew. "Sorry, I didn't mean to make you uncomfortable. It's just that I don't want to cross any boundaries, being the late comer to the group, you know."

"No, I'm sorry. I didn't mean to say it like that. I'm in survival mode. I'm not looking for a boyfriend."

"I understand."

"How about you? Do you have a wife or girlfriend that was left . . . ?" There was no good way to talk about it.

Ray did not answer right away. He looked into the park-like environment. "I was engaged. Danielle was her name. I miss her."

"Maybe she made it," Sarah said, sensing his sadness. "Is it possible?"

Ray shook his head. "I was talking to her when I saw those things break into her bedroom and attack her. But I was on the space station, and there was nothing I could do to help her."

"I'm sorry," Sarah said, feeling sad for him having to watch such an awful scene.

Ray leaned forward and looked toward the ground.

Sarah leaned over and gave him a hug. Ray hugged her back. It felt good. Part of her wanted to stay in the warm embrace, but she pulled away, not wanting things to go any further.

"Mom."

Sarah jumped, not expecting Willis to be standing right behind her. She turned around. "What?"

"When will things be turned back on?"

"It's only been fifteen minutes. I thought you were playing cards."

"We are, but we want to go into the holodeck."

Ray stood up. "I'll go up and see how Artie is doing, but I think it's still going to be awhile."

"Okay, thanks," Willis said.

Sarah watched Ray walk away and then looked back at Willis who was holding back a laugh.

"What's so funny?"

"You've got two boyfriends."

Sarah shook her head and stood up. "I don't have any boyfriends. I'm going back to my room to rest. You should go back to your card game."

"You can deny it, Mom, but both Ray and Jack like you."

"Enough of that, mister," Sarah said, walking out of the greenhouse with Willis. "Wake me up if I'm still sleeping when things get turned back on."

"I will." Willis began walking back to the others and then stopped. He turned back to his mom. "Who are you going to pick?"

"Wouldn't you like to know?"

SEVEN

Jack fell to his hands and knees and began clawing his way to higher ground as it rolled and vibrated underneath him. The ledge crumbled and fell into the black pit as the rocks they had removed from the ship went over the rim, barely missing him.

"Sarah," Jack shouted as the quake ceased and he found stable ground. "Can you hear me?"

Jack sat down, exhausted from the struggle of climbing to safety and grateful for the water-cooled underwear. He could not believe what was happening. Jack was alone on a crumbling rim of some gigantic crater on the far side of the moon. He had no idea how the others had fared on their way to the bottom of the basin. To his knowledge, the ship had not flown out of the crater so it must still be down there. Not only that, but it was getting darker and he had no idea how to operate the suit he wore. There were buttons and knobs on the chest, arms, and helmet, but he was afraid to press any of them for fear he may accidentally disengage the bubble around his head, or some such thing.

However, the dire situation that Jack faced was juxtaposed with the beauty around him. The black sky and rocky rim were both dreadful and awe-inspiring.

But now what? What if the unthinkable had happened and everyone had perished? God forbid. Jack saw no way to get down to them and could not see any lights from the ship. What about the suit's oxygen; when would it run low? Now that he was not moving debris off the ship's shield or running for his life, he had time to notice the display at the bottom of his visual field. It appeared the oxygen was at thirty-eight percent. How could it be so low already? There was little time to figure out a way to survive. If it was even possible to devise a survival plan.

No matter how he looked at it, he had to do something and do it now. The oxygen would eventually run out. Maybe the cooling suit would quit working and his helmet would fog up; he would not be able to see where he was going. If that was to happen, how would he wipe it when he could not reach inside the helmet? He would be blind. Before all that happened, he needed a plan but there were essentially no options. All he saw that he could do was to stay where he was at and hope that they would soon come to his rescue. It was not like there was a town he could walk to or a trucker driving by that he could hitch a ride with. He was alone, and possibly the only person alive on the moon. Well, at least it would be better dying this way than by being eaten by zombies, moss with teeth, or the crazed mutant monsters. But would suffocating and freezing to death really be better? There was no good way to die.

While Jack waited for inspiration or words of wisdom from on high to come to his rescue, he thought of Sarah and her boys. Did he love her? Yes, he decided. He had never told her. Now it was too late.

"I never thought I'd die like this," Jack said, looking down at the suit encasing his body. He did not want to live when everyone else was dead. What was the point of being the only human left alive? None. He was the last earthling left alive, and the human species would die with him.

Where was God?

Jack looked at the oxygen level now at thirty-seven percent. What the hell. He crawled slowly to the edge of the drop-off and looked down into the pit, hoping that maybe there was some sign of Infinity One, or at least see that damned robot climbing up the slope to rescue him. There was nothing. No sign of life.

He looked toward the upper part of the crater's rim. Maybe they had flown out during the chaos of the moonquake. Maybe the dust obscured the sight of the ship flying away and landing somewhere outside the crater. He would need to climb to a higher elevation to see.

As Jack climbed, he watched the oxygen drop one digit at a time. It all seemed so useless, but he was not giving up. He took it slow, not wanting to tumble backward and into the depth of the basin.

When he finally reached the top, he looked out over the rugged terrain. Protecting his psyche, he mused that he was king of the hill and emperor of the moon. His kingdom was desolate, however. Where had all his subjects gone? There was no Infinity One. It must not have made it.

Then a ding, like that of a car's gas gauge indicating low fuel, sounded in his ear. His oxygen was at ten percent. Shit.

Jack dropped to his knees. He felt like he was kneeling before the celestial altar of a God that had abandoned him and the others. How could God allow Sarah, the kids, and everyone else onboard the ship to die after all they had fought through?

Then a glimmer of light caught his attention. Was it the sun reflecting off some weird rock formation? He focused on it. If it was something natural, it had a uniform shape, like that of a pyramid.

Jack kept staring at it. Was he hallucinating because his oxygen level was dropping? Or could Tony have been right after all and there really was an alien base nearby? He would check it out. What did he have to lose? He could die where he was—an absolute certainty—or die checking out the damned thing. He would go for it.

He walked down the other side of the rim. As he got closer, despair turned to hope.

"Damn, Tony, you were right."

Jack picked up his pace as he approached the pyramid. It was obviously manmade—or alien made—with a shiny surface, like polished limestone. Whoever made it did not get the material from the moon. It reminded Jack of the Egyptian pyramids, but much smaller.

Reflective lights outlined the face of the pyramid with a closed door. Was anyone inside? It did not matter. The oxygen alarm was constantly sounding at a level of two percent, and he was having difficulty breathing.

Jack stood in front of the door but saw no way to open it. He frantically ran his hands along the surface and around the frame, but there was no noticeable handles, knobs, or buttons.

Now at one percent, he felt like a flopping fish out of water with its gills flaring, trying to take in oxygen. He began banging on the door, yelling for someone to open the godforsaken thing.

Then, to his surprise, it opened. He wobbled inside, and it closed behind him. He was in a chamber, but that was all he noticed as he tried to figure out how to take the helmet off. He fumbled around the neck ring until he could remove it. The oxygen dropped to zero. He fell to the floor, suffocating.

Jack gasped, pulling musty air into his lungs, but it did not matter. Oxygen was oxygen. He was weak and about to pass out as he turned onto his back.

Moments later, Jack's respirations slowed as breathing became easier. He looked around the enclosed space. He might have bought himself time, but he was also trapped on the moon. Alone. In a place where no one would ever find him.

EIGHT

Sarah woke to a gentle hum and cheers of joy. Infinity One was powering on. She sat up, caught her bearings, and walked out of the cabin. The kids were sitting in the lounge, laughing with excitement.

"Do those chairs have seatbelts?" Sarah said.

They looked at the sides of the chairs.

"Yeah, right here," Georgie said, pulling out the strap.

"Be prepared to put them on because we may be getting ready to liftoff and find Jack," Sarah said, running a hand through her hair as she walked to the ladder.

When Sarah reached the flight deck, it was calm. Ray was seated in the captain's chair with both Max and the professor at his side. She walked up and stood next to Tony, who was standing behind the control desk, watching.

"Is Infinity One recharged?" Sarah asked.

"Yep," Tony said.

"Artie, engage the cloaking shield," Ray said.

"Cloaking shield engaged, Ray."

Ray looked at Tony and then at Sarah. "We'll look for Jack."

"Have you gotten a signal on him, yet?" Tony said.

"No," Ray said, turning back toward the monitors. "There's still a malfunction in the sensors. Artie is working on it."

"Don't those suits at least have a beacon like black boxes in jets?"

"Yes, they do. But like I said, something is malfunctioning."

"When are we going to look for Jack?" Sarah asked.

"Right now," Ray said. "Artie, are we ready to elevate?"

"Infinity One is ready, Ray."

"So far, I still don't see the alien ship," Max said.

Ray's voice boomed through the ship's loudspeakers. "Everyone, strap in. I am getting us out of this hole, and we'll look for Jack."

Sarah and Tony buckled into the flight seats as the ship rose and slowly ascended to the top of the basin.

"That's where we were before we fell to the crater floor," the professor said, pointing to a collapsed shelf as Ray rotated the ship. "Keep an eye out for Jack."

"I don't see him," Max said. He adjusted his glasses and looked at Ray. "Try and talk to him."

"There's no connection, but I'll try," Ray said, speaking into the microphone. "Jack, can you hear me?"

Silence.

"Jack, this is Ray, can you hear me?"

Past the forward window lay the rubble on the rim where Jack had once stood.

"Artie, any sign of Jack?"

"Negative, Ray."

"Maybe he walked to the alien base," Tony said, unstrapping.

"Tony, there aren't any alien moon bases on the—" Max stopped speaking when he saw the pyramid. "Well, I'll be damned."

"There aren't any tracks," Ray said. "He didn't go there."

"Maybe the tracks were affected by a coronal mass ejection," the professor said. "It's possible the dust was displaced by solar wind particles, thus removing his footprints."

"Highly unlikely," Ray said. "A vacuum surrounds the moon. He's probably buried underneath—"

Panicked, Sarah removed the safety harness and walked up to the control desk. "Send Artie out to look for him. Jack could be dying underneath those rocks. We have to save him."

Ray answered without looking at her. "If he's buried, he's already gone. Every time we send Artie outside the ship, we risk losing him. If that were to happen, my ability to manage Infinity One would be totally limited, possibly leading to our own deaths. Are you willing to risk that?"

"We're not leaving Jack behind," Tony said. "I'll go out if you won't send the cyborg."

Ray dropped his head and then looked up. "You're wasting your time."

Tony's stance widened. "Why? If Jack wasn't crushed, he could still be alive. We weren't powered down that long; his suit could still have oxygen."

Ray shook his head. "His suit was low on oxygen, and I'm sure it would be depleted by now."

"What?" Sarah could not believe what she was hearing. "You put Jack in a suit with hardly any oxygen? Why did you do that?"

"As I said at the time, I knew the suit would fit him and was safe to use. His oxygen would have been fine while he was helping Artie. I didn't plan for the moonquake to happen."

"Set this thing down and help me suit up, Ray," Tony said, walking to the airlock. "I'm going out there."

"Have it your way. But your life is in your own hands." Ray landed Infinity One on the shelf near where Jack had last been.

Sarah watched as Ray helped Tony put on the spacesuit. Tony was tall, but Ray found a suit that fit him. "What's the oxygen level?"

"One-hundred percent," Ray said, swiftly sealing Tony's suit.

Tony exited the ship and walked to where Jack was last seen. He kept calling for Jack as he moved rocks like Goliath, working for over an hour before sitting down for a break. Moments later he was back at work, digging through the rubble for close to six hours before Ray convinced him he was fighting a losing battle.

Sarah fought back tears as Tony came back into the airlock. She turned to Ray who was walking up to her. He put his arms around her and pulled her close as tears streamed down her cheeks and onto his T-shirt. They had already discussed the possibility of Jack having fallen over the edge to his death, but she would not be satisfied until they found his body.

Tony doffed the spacesuit in the equipment airlock and came onto the flight deck. "Ray, let's go to the alien base. If Jack saw the lights, he would have gone there."

Ray released Sarah and walked back to the captain's seat. "Even if he saw it and decided to go there, he wouldn't have made it. But we'll go there, anyway. Strap in, you know my ability to maneuver isn't the greatest, even though I didn't do too bad last time."

"That's what you say," Max said.

Ray lifted the ship off the ledge and hovered over the surface, guiding it toward the pyramid.

"See, Professor," Tony said from the back of the room. "An alien moon base, right there before your eyes."

The professor was about to answer when alarms began to sound.

"The aliens are back," Max said.

With inhuman calmness, Artie said, "That is correct, Max. An alien ship has passed Earth and is headed toward the moon."

"I thought the cloaking shield was on," Max said, testing his safety harness.

"Shit, it's not at one-hundred percent." Ray kept the ship suspended above the moon's surface and switched on the loudspeaker. "If you're not secured in a seat, do it now."

"The alien craft has detected us and is coming our way," Artie said. "Engaging the force field."

"Thank you, Artie. Prepare to jump."

"Jump?" Max said. "Don't tell me you plan on scrambling us like eggs in a frying pan."

"I thought the wormhole technology hasn't been used yet," the professor said.

"Brace for incoming fire," Artie said.

Infinity One vibrated like a bell being struck with a metal hammer.

"The force field is failing, Ray," Artie said.

"Fire the laser gun, now, Artie."

"Laser away. Direct impact. No detectable damage to the alien vessel."

"Incoming," Artie said.

This time Infinity One jolted violently from the hit.

"One more hit will have serious consequences, Ray. I advise jumping, immediately."

"Now, now! Through the wormhole, Artie," Ray said, bracing himself.

At that moment, Sarah saw everything turn into a slow-motion blur. Then silence. She felt like she was melting into the chair, her molecules mixing with the molecules of everything her body touched, becoming one. Terror filled her, but she realized she could think so her mind must be intact. Or maybe it was her soul that was intact and her body turning into mush. She could no longer focus on the surrounding people. She wanted it to end. Then there was a whoosh. It seemed that everything was catching up as alarms sounded and lights flashed.

NINE

Sarah was afraid to look down at her body as she moved a hand off the armrest. It was not attached.

"What the hell, Ray," Max said, examining his hands. "I was able to reach right through this table. My hand could've been stuck in the metal like sailors in the Philadelphia experiment who ended up fused to the bulkhead of the USS Eldridge."

"It only appeared that way," Ray said, silencing the alarms. "You're perfectly fine."

"How can you be so sure since you've never done this before?"

Ray gave a sideways glance. "Because you're the same cranky bastard you always are."

"Where are we?" Sarah said, releasing her harness.

Outside the forward window was a glowing blue planet orbiting a red sun.

"Looks like we're in the Alpha Centauri star system," the professor said, looking at a map of stars, constellations, and galaxies.

"Correct, Professor," Artie said. "We are near the red dwarf star Proxima Centauri in the triple star system Alpha Centauri in the constellation Centaurus. The planet is Proxima b."

"It looks almost like Earth, except that it has a bit of a glow," Sarah said, walking up to the control desk.

"Great," Max said. "We just left that red man-eating moss on Earth, now we've come to a planet with blue glowing moss."

"Calm down, Max," the professor said. "The planet is in the Goldilocks zone so it's possible it could be habitable. Except that it is rather close the red dwarf which is a flare star and could send outbursts of radiation toward Proxima b."

"It looks like it has life," Sarah said. "It's blue."

"Artie, is the planet fit for humans?" Ray said, turning to look at the android still standing on top of the pedestal in the center of the flight deck.

"Proxima b has a strong magnetic field and is able to deflect damaging solar flares that may erupt from Proxima Centauri. Human life can be sustained, Ray."

"Is there life on the planet right now?"

"Yes, Ray. I detect vegetation and life forms, but I am currently unable to provide details. My instrumentation is limited until repairs are made."

"Artie, give me a status report."

"The alien vessel did not follow us through the wormhole. Damage to Infinity One is minimal and repairable. The force field and the cloaking shield are unusable until recharged. There were no fatalities."

"Fatalities?" Max said. "My faith in this ship and its captain are waning."

"I didn't know Artie could tell how we were doing physically," Sarah said.

Ray swiveled his chair and looked at Sarah. "If everyone would put on a wristband Artie could do a better job at making sure everyone is safe and healthy."

"How's the professor's blood pressure?" Max said, challenging Artie's skills.

"I only have general data until the band is placed on the body. Professor Dillon is alive."

Max grumbled and looked back at the space vista. "None of us are going to wear those damned bands."

"I'm going below," Sarah said, meeting Clare at the ladder.

"Everyone's fine down there," Clare said. She walked up next to Tony. "Wow, that's . . . amazing, awesome, spectacular. I don't know how to describe it."

"Will the aliens be able to find us?" Tony asked.

"I don't think so," Ray said. "They would've had to of latched onto our tail to follow us through, and that didn't happen. But like I've said—"

"We know," Max interrupted. "You're only the test pilot."

"Ray, I found a suitable place to land Infinity One so that I can commence on the repairs," Artie said.

"Send me the coordinates."

"With our luck," Max said. "This is the planet that Rausuca and the aliens are from."

"Or the reptilians," Tony said.

Ray broadcast another order through the ship to strap in while Infinity One punctured through puffy white clouds and sat down—after a couple rotations—in a clearing between blue trees, next to a lake.

"The air is breathable, and no threats are detected," Artie said.

"No one should go outside until we search the place for hostiles," Tony said. "It looks peaceful, but looks can be deceiving."

Ray powered down the ship. "I agree. But I need to inspect the ship's exterior and assess the safety of our location."

"Is the equipment airlock safe to go into?" Tony asked, walking to the door.

"Why?" Ray said.

"I want to get Jack's alien pistol. It should still be in your locker."

Ray looked at Tony and then nodded.

Tony went into the airlock and opened the compartment where Jack had put his clothes. He lifted the jeans, thinking the pistol was hidden underneath. It was not. He looked through everything in the locker. The pistol was nowhere to be found.

"The handgun's not in there," Tony said, walking out of the airlock. "Anyone know where it's at?"

"Could he have taken it with him?" Clare said. She walked into the airlock and did her own search.

"Do you know, Ray?" Tony said. "Did Jack take it with him?"

"I didn't see him take it, but he could have grabbed it when I wasn't looking."

"I don't remember seeing it in his hand." Tony looked at Clare who was coming out of the airlock. "Did you find it?"

"Nope. I don't like having one of the weapons come up missing."

"Me either." Tony looked at the captain's seat and suspiciously at the back of Ray's head. Then he looked at the M16 hanging over the back of Ray's chair. "I'll use Ray's rifle when I go outside. Is that all right, Ray?"

"I'm using it." Ray spun the chair around until he faced Tony. "I'm going outside."

"You can use my pistol." The professor handed Tony both the gun and the hip holster.

"That only leaves us Sarah's wand," Clare said. "Other than Willis and Georgie, she's the only one who can use it. She'll have to go with you guys."

"There has to be weapons on this ship," Tony said. "I find it hard to believe they built a ship with a laser gun, a cloaking shield, and a force field but didn't supply the crew with any type of firearm to defend themselves."

"Infinity One wasn't ready for space travel when we took off," Ray said. "If you recall, we were forced into using it because of that creeping crud and those mutants. So, don't get on your high horse and act like I'm hiding something."

Tony did not say anything.

Ray got on the loudspeaker. "Sarah, can you come up to the flight deck, please? And bring the wand."

Moments later Sarah stepped off the ladder. "What's going on?"

Clare adjusted her camo cap. "Since you're the only one that thing likes, we need you to go outside with Tony and Ray to check out the area. Just need to make sure it's safe. Are you okay with that?"

"Oh, sure. When are we doing this?"

Ray stood up. "Artie, is it safe to leave the ship?"

"Yes, Ray."

"What about the robot?" Tony said. "Is it coming with us?"

Ray walked to the airlock. "He has repairs to make. I'll send him out later."

"Let's do it, then," Tony said, following Sarah and Ray into the equipment room.

The door closed behind them. Then they went into the crew airlock, and Ray closed the door. They stood facing the airtight exit door.

Ray looked at Sarah. "Are you ready?"

"As ready as I'll ever be."

TEN

Jack stood alone in the middle of the pyramid's stone chamber, holding the helmet in his hand, wishing he had brought the alien pistol. Enough light emitted from—somewhere—allowing him the ability to see what appeared to be Egyptian hieroglyphs carved into the walls. It reminded him of the alien spaceship, the black boxes, and the cargo that he had the unfortunate luck of witnessing. Max might be able to decipher it, but it was nothing more than jumbled symbols to him.

It was evident that no one had been in the place for a long time because he was the only one that had disturbed the dust on the floor. On the one hand, he was relieved he did not have to deal with killer moon men, but on the other hand, he was more alone than ever. But at least he was in a chamber with oxygen. Even so, he still had to find a door, other than the one he came in.

Jack felt along the walls, feeling the etchings, and admiring the smoothness of the handiwork. He realized the hieroglyphs were not carved by someone with a chisel and mallet, but with expert precision. Not surprising since whoever could build a pyramid on the moon obviously had to be far more advanced than any human alive.

Then he stopped when he heard stone sliding behind him. Without delay, he put the helmet on and turned around, fearing the door that was opening led to the outside airless environment. But instead, it was a different door—an interior entry.

As Jack began taking off his helmet, it was then that he realized he could breathe with it on. He looked at the oxygen level and noticed it was rising. It must draw oxygen from the environment to replenish itself. But if that was the case, shouldn't it have been fully charged when he first put on the suit inside the ship? The high-tech suit would certainly be able to sustain a person for longer than it had him. It must be malfunctioning, but at least it would hold oxygen as backup if he needed it, and possibly save his life.

Breathing a sigh of relief, Jack took off his helmet. He examined the dials and buttons on the arms of the suit. He noticed one was a symbol of a flashlight, so he pressed it and a small beam of light shot from the cuff of the suit. Not the easiest to shine around the room, but still it was useable.

Jack walked up to the opening and saw a compartment; it was an elevator.

"Great," Jack said. The elevator had to go down. He was not so sure he wanted to go underground and make his location even less detectable to anyone with the ability to find him.

He stood in front of the lift, trying to decide whether to go into it and see where it took him, or wait until his suit's oxygen was refilled and walk back to where Infinity One had sat before it fell off the edge of the crater.

There was no guarantee that if he went to where the elevator took him that it would bring him back if he changed his mind and wanted to keep looking for the others. But, of course, there was the obvious truth that he had a defective suit and would die at the crater's rim, looking for the others, while the oxygen dropped. Maybe he would not be so lucky to reach the pyramid again. It was a long walk.

The fact was, he could not stay where he was; he had to decide.

"What the hell."

Jack stepped into the elevator. It did not move. Maybe it was not an elevator. Maybe it was a coffin, a death box, a trap. Jack was about to step off when the door closed and he felt the sense of motion. He was moving. Moments later the door opened.

Before him was a large open room with a fifteen-foot-high giant ring toward the back. It reminded Jack of the fictional Stargates he had seen on television. However, if it was a portal that allowed people to transport to distant locations, it was not activated.

If it was a Stargate, the idea was easy to swallow. After all, he had been through a portal in the prepper compound and through the one on the Mars base. The technology was real, but where did it go and how was it activated?

Jack stepped off the elevator. He felt so small in the pyramid-shaped base. The part seen on the moon's surface was only the tip of the iceberg. Next to the walls—painted with colorful life-sized images of people with headdress and other Egyptian type symbols—were a series of what appeared to be tombs. Dozens of them. At the rate Jack's luck was going, he envisioned ravenous mummies rising from them, ready to attack the intruder. But it was quiet. The only sound was his steps as he walked up to the large broad square stone plinth, in the center of the room, supporting steps that led to a slender pedestal, like a music stand, with a control panel consisting of two concentric circles of symbols.

He climbed the steps and stood in front of the stand. The panel had a series of symbols partially hidden underneath undisturbed grime. The symbols were similar yet different from the ones he had seen associated with the aliens. So, if this device was not from the aliens—the bad aliens—was it from the good aliens?

Jack walked off the platform and over to the tombs. When he got closer, he realized they were not sarcophaguses, but more like hibernation units. The lit panels on each ones' top appeared to be functioning. He could not see inside, and he was not about to press any of the buttons.

Then it occurred to him, and he did not necessarily like the thought, that when an intruder came into a room where beings were in stasis, one of them should wake up to assess the threat. Of course, that was in the movies, not in real life.

Nevertheless, Jack looked around the room. Nothing moved. Everything looked like it had when he first walked inside.

Relieved, Jack continued investigating. He hoped to find another door, a door with another option for escape. He found none.

"Well, I can't stay here," Jack said, walking back up to the pedestal. He studied the panel. Nothing made sense.

"Where are you, Max, when I need you?" Then grief overtook him. Max was gone, so was everyone else, at least as far as he knew.

Jack swiped his hand over the panel like Sarah was able to do on the alien spaceship. Nothing happened. "I guess my genes are from the wrong side of the tracks."

He sighed. Even if he could get the gate to open, he could not go through it until he knew for sure the fate of the others. He looked at the oxygen level on his suit, it was almost entirely charged.

"I've got to look for them." Jack knew the attempt would be futile.

He went back to the elevator and up to the surface. He put on his helmet—hoping he had put it on correctly—and stepped out of the pyramid and into the barren moon landscape. He rechecked the oxygen and walked back to the rim. He had never felt more alone.

ELEVEN

Ray opened the outer door. Sarah braced for suffocation, ready to reach for the supplemental oxygen secured to the airlock wall. But instead, what she breathed in was a sweet floral scent, like a cottage flower garden after a spring rain shower.

"Stay close to me," Ray said, directing his comment to Sarah.

Sarah held the alien wand in her hand as she followed Ray down the sloping platform to the sand that lined their side of the deep blue lake. Tony brought up the rear.

An eerily beautiful rose colored sun shined above the horizon, casting a warm glow over the blue and black vegetation.

Ray took soil and plant samples as they walked to the lake. When they reached the shore, he filled a test tube with water and put it into the shoulder bag he carried. "I'll have Artie run a complete analysis on these."

"So far the planet looks livable," Sarah said.

"Looks can be deceiving," Tony said. "Stay on guard."

They turned around and looked back at Infinity One. There was no apparent damage. Other than the cracking sound of the hull as it cooled, everything looked intact.

"Let's walk around it," Ray said, walking back toward the ship.

Tony stopped. "Did you hear that?"

Sarah looked back at Tony. "Hear what?"

Tony raised a hand. "Shh. Listen."

A distant, barely audible, repetitious drumming could be heard inland.

"It's coming from the foot of that mountain."

"I wonder what it is?"

Tony put a hand on the pistol. "It's probably a warning drumbeat. There are people on this planet."

Tony shouted up to Ray who had continued walking. "Ray, I thought that robot gave the all clear."

Ray continued inspecting the ship as he spoke. "He did. I wouldn't worry about it unless it gets closer. It could just be some weird planet noise like wind blowing through a cave or something."

The three scouts continued to walk around the spacecraft until they were back where they started.

"The ship looks undamaged," Ray said. He looked toward the blue forest. "I don't hear that sound anymore."

They went back inside the ship.

Max walked up to them. "Well, how is it out there?"

"It's beautiful," Sarah said. "You'll have to check it out."

"I'll check it out as soon as I know I won't be eaten by some blue monster."

Ray walked up to the lab table equipped with a microscope, fume hood, and various other equipment. "I'm going to run the soil and water samples, Artie. How are you coming on the repairs?"

"Repairs for the cloaking shield and force field are almost complete. Recharging the warp drive will take approximately twenty-three hours, Ray."

"Can we go outside?" Willis said, standing with the eager kids.

"When it's safe, you can go out," Sarah said.

"I am engaging the force field," Artie said. "I have it set to extend one-hundred feet from the hull."

"If the kids go outside, what happens if they accidentally touch the protective field?" Sarah said.

Ray placed the final sample into an analyzer, washed his hands, and walked up to Sarah. "Nothing happens if you're inside the field; it just feels a little spongy. But if you're on the outside, it could shock you, depending on the level of protection that is set."

"Does that mean we can leave the ship?" Father Mitch asked.

Ray looked at the analyzers and the green lights. "So far everything looks harmless with the samples. It should be all right."

Sarah followed the kids and dogs as they ran through the open airlock doors, stopping when they reached the ramp. The landscape was so unbelievable that it was more than the brain could absorb at one time. But moments later the kids were walking down the ramp, oohing and aahing at the sights.

"At least we can see where the force field is," Georgie said.

To Sarah, the field looked like a red-rimmed glass bowl that had been turned upside down, except that the view through it was clear and not warped or distorted. The red rim that circled the ship acted as a fence so that people would not be running into it.

From the ramp, Sarah looked back inside the ship and saw the professor walking over to Ray and the workstation while Max walked up to her.

"I'm sorry about Jack." Max sounded genuinely sorrowful.

Sarah's heart sank. She had forgotten about the disaster—if only for moment—but now it was back. "I'm not giving up on finding him, Max. He could still be alive. I'm sure of it."

Max did not say anything, he only nodded. Then he looked back at the ship. "Artie, make sure you don't leave without us."

"I will not leave without the crew, Max."

Max leaned toward Sarah and whispered, "Yeah, like I believe that. Now, let's check this place out."

Sarah put a hand to her nose. "When we go back inside, you need to pick yourself out a room. They have everything you need in there. They're actually quite nice."

"Are you trying to tell me something?" Max grinned.

Sarah shook her head and smiled as she and Max walked down the ramp.

"We need a couple lawn chairs," Max said, twisting his back. It cracked.

"Listen," Sarah said. "I hear that sound again."

"I don't hear anything."

"Off in the distance."

"Oh, yeah, it sounds like a manmade sound, like tom-toms."

"I think it's louder than when we were out here earlier."

"That's not good, no matter what's causing it."

TWELVE

Max started back up the ramp. "I'm letting the others know."

Sarah watched the kids and dogs run and play as if they were in elementary school. They seemed happy, jubilant. Moments later Max walked down the ramp stamping his feet.

"What's wrong?" Sarah said.

"They found a problem."

"Another problem? What is it?"

"That damned robot can't repair the ship unless we find some type of crystal."

"Crystal?"

"Yeah, a rare dilithium crystal."

"Where are we going to find that?"

"They're searching to see if there's any on this planet. Tony and Clare are downstairs checking the food supply."

Sarah and Max walked back into the ship. The professor was seated at the control desk next to Ray, engrossed in a screen.

Father walked up to them. "Max told you the news?"

"Yeah."

Sarah saw Ray turn and look at her. "You probably already know that we need a dilithium crystal for Artie to finish the repairs and restore the warp drive."

"What happens if we can't find any?"

"Then we're stuck on this planet."

Max sat down in the copilot seat. "At least this planet is better than Earth. There's no man-eating moss or aliens around."

Sarah rubbed her forehead. "I'm okay with living on another planet, but I want to go back and look for Jack."

"He's dead," Ray said.

"You don't know that," Sarah said. "We haven't found his body. He could still be alive."

Ray did not say anything but instead turned back to the console.

"Ray?" Artie said.

"Yes, what is it, Artie."

"I have located a dilithium crystal five miles east from here."

"Will we be able to carry it?"

"It is basketball sized. I will need to carry it back to the ship. Its weight would be tiring for humans to carry over a long distance."

"Whoever goes to get the crystal will be heading right toward the drumbeat," Max said. "Hey, Artie."

"Yes, Max."

"What's making that sound coming from the direction of the mountain range?"

"I am having difficulty assessing the sound. The backup systems give detecting dilithium crystals a high priority. Until we load the fuel into the warp drive, I am not fully functional."

"Ray, are the results back on the samples you took?" Sarah said.

"Preliminary results show that they're not toxic. If we're not able to get the crystal, then we'll need to come up with a better name for this planet other than Proxima b because it'll be our new home sweet home. We'll be castaways like Robinson Crusoe."

"Robinson Crusoe on Mars," Father said.

"More like Gilligan's Island, if you ask me," Max said.

Tony stepped off the ladder and walked across the flight deck. "What's going on?"

"Don't take off your gun belt," Sarah said. "We have a little trip to take."

THIRTEEN

The spacesuit seemed to be holding its oxygen. So well, in fact, that it indicated there was twelve hours' worth of breathing left. That would be enough time to walk down the side of the crater—at least part of the way—so that he could see if Infinity One was on the crater floor. Hopefully, it had its exterior lights turned on and was not hidden in a dark shadow.

The sun was now angled so that he had a better view of the crater. He could see where part of the rim had collapsed and so far, there was no sign of the ship. He was not sure whether to be happy that the ship had somehow escaped or sad that it was buried and damaged, leaving everyone on board either injured or worse yet, dead.

Jack kept going until the oxygen was almost half gone. He had better turn back; going up would use more oxygen. He was angry at Ray for leaving him. When—or if—he saw Ray again, a fist to his face was in order.

When Jack reached the pyramid, he fumbled around for the way to open the door. Finally, it opened, and he went inside. Jack took off the helmet and went back down to the nonfunctioning Stargate and hibernation tombs. He walked up to the pedestal, which he assumed controlled the portal, but he still could not get it to power on. It was dead.

He sat down on the top step of the platform. His stomach growled. How long had it been since he last ate or drank anything? Too long.

"Now what?" Jack said aloud. "Well, I could curl up like a little baby and go to sleep until the Grim Reaper comes and takes me away." That actually sounded like a good idea.

"I could keep recharging the spacesuit with oxygen and keep going outside looking for the others or at least set outside the pyramid hoping they will see me when they come to rescue me." Yeah right.

"I could keep messing with the Stargate controls until I find the right combination." That could take thousands of years.

"Or." Jack looked at one of the hibernation beds. "I could wake up whatever is inside one of those things and have them help me get out of here. If the thing kills me, well, I'm going to die anyway. Might as well go out with a bang."

Jack walked over to the chamber closest to him. He had walked around them before and saw no sign of which one may be the leader of these things. He examined the panel. "Maybe I can't open this either."

Keeping his helmet in one hand, just in case he had to make a mad dash outside, he pushed the first lit hieroglyph that looked like a looped piece of rope. The chamber began hissing. He stepped away.

"Oh my god, it's going to open. I hope I did the right thing."

Jack's heart raced as he backed toward the elevator. Then he stopped when the lid slid into the side of the casket. From where he was at, he could not see inside. He waited for the thing inside the tomb to rise. Should he walk toward it or wait? He waited.

Deciding that it must be dead—it had to have been locked in that thing for a long time—he crept up to it. Then he stopped when he saw the top of its head come into view. He hesitated to go any further, fearing its hideous face would make him faint like a little girl, but he had to see what was lying inside the crypt.

No other hibernation beds were opening, so he took one baby step forward. It had white hair. One more step. He saw its eyes. One more step forward. He saw its face. His breath left him as if he had been punched in the chest.

FOURTEEN

Hues of red and magenta saturated the evening sky, prompting the scout team to leave the next morning. When dawn came, the crew was awakened by peaceful sounds of the gentle flow of water and songbirds.

"It is time for everyone to rise." Artie's soothing voice was heard throughout the ship. "Today is Thursday, December twenty-third. Proxima b time is five am. Selected crew members need to prepare for the ten-mile round trip to retrieve the crystal."

Sarah did not want to get out of the soft, warm bed; but she did. She got up, took a shower, and put on her clean clothes that she had washed in the ship's laundry room. Sarah walked out of her cabin and saw people sitting in the dining area eating and talking. The aroma of bacon, eggs, and coffee made it seem as though she was back home. When she looked toward the greenhouse, she saw the red dwarf star breaking the horizon. She was anywhere but home.

"Hey, Mom," Willis said. "The space food tastes great. You should try it."

Sarah went to the wall housing the food dispenser and ordered herself a cup of black coffee and two slices of buttered toast. Within seconds it was delivered to the compartment in front of her. She took it and walked to the table, sitting between Ray and Max.

"Good to see you finally took off those coveralls," Sarah said, looking at the black goth clothes partially obscured by a black hooded sweatshirt.

Max dipped a slice of toast in the yoke. "I'm getting used to them."

"Good morning, sunshine," Ray said from her other side. "Ready for the journey?"

She turned toward Ray. His hair was slicked back, and he smelled of a quality cologne. "I suppose."

Clare pushed her empty plate to the side. "Ray, don't forget to show me how to use the ship's laser gun before you leave."

"I will."

"I have a name for the planet that's better than Proxima b," Georgie said.

"What'd you come up with?" Sarah said.

"You know how the plants are colored blue and black? Well, I think Blue on Black is what we should call it."

"Don't you mean black and blue?" Max said.

"No, Blue on Black like the song by the Kenny Wayne Shepherd Band."

Max gave Georgie a strange look. "You're proposing we name this blue ball after a song?"

"Sure, why not?"

"I like it," Clare said. She picked up her empty plate and walked to the food station's dishwasher. "So when are you guys leaving?"

"As soon as everyone's ready," Ray said.

"I'm ready," Tony said.

"I wish I could go with you," Georgie said. "But I don't have my sword."

"You guys need to take care of the ship while we're gone," Sarah said.

The professor held back a burp, then said, "Will we be able to communicate with you while you're gone?"

"You can talk to me and Artie," Ray said. "Sarah and Tony will need to put on the safety wristbands. They can receive and transmit data so that we can talk to each other and the ship can track us."

"I'm not putting that thing on," Tony said. "They're for prisoners."

"Don't be ridiculous," Ray said. "They're not for inmates."

"Do they come off?" Tony asked, putting the last bite of egg into his mouth.

"Of course, you can take it off whenever you want," Ray said.

"I'll try it," Willis said, rising from his seat.

"No, you're not," Sarah said. "The Walmart kids and Randy were stuck wearing bands, and they were either prisoners or people the aliens wanted to control."

"Good ol' Randolph Watson," Max said. "I wonder what that character is up to these days."

Ray glanced at Max and then looked at Sarah. "These are not the same bands. I recommend using them."

"I'll think about it," Sarah said.

"Besides, why would they put prisoner bands on a deep-space craft? This isn't a prisoner transport ship." Ray wiped his mouth with a paper napkin and stood up. "If you're not going to wear one, then I advise staying close to me. We don't know what's out there."

"I'll be right at your side."

Tony looked at Ray's wrists. "Why aren't you wearing one?"

Ray held up his hand. "I have the implant. I'm always wearing one."

"Let's head out, then," Tony said. "I don't want to get caught walking in the dark on the way back."

Ray called for Artie.

"Yes, Ray," Artie said through the ship's speaker system.

"We're ready to leave."

"The gear is available and in the equipment airlock."

"Gear?" Tony said. "What are we taking?"

"Backpacks with survival stuff," Ray said.

They all got up from the table and walked to the elevator. Ray stopped in front of the supplemental oxygen and the safety bands. He opened the see-through case, took out a band and slipped it onto his wrist.

"Watch," Ray said, taking it off. "It also monitors your vital signs."

Sarah took a bracelet from the case and examined it. "It doesn't look exactly like the prisoner bracelets."

"I still wouldn't put it on," Tony said.

"If I put it on and it doesn't come off, I'm not going."

Ray crossed his arms. "Okay."

Sarah was not sure what to do, but she trusted Ray. She slipped it on as people gasped. Then she pulled it off without difficulty.

"See," Ray said. "I understand your hesitancy, but there's nothing to worry about."

"I still don't trust it," Tony said, climbing up the ladder.

Sarah put the band back on. Ray showed her how to use it as they rode the elevator up to the flight deck.

"Test that bracelet," Clare said, walking to the command console with the professor and Max.

Sarah walked in the equipment room where Artie had three backpacks setting out. "Can you hear me?"

"It's registering loud and clear," Clare said. "Ray, show us how to use the ship's laser gun."

While Ray gave instructions on the utilization of the weapon, Artie walked up to Sarah. "I am reading you as well and will not let any harm come to you."

"Thank you, Artie."

"I can see your location and vital signs on the screen," Max said. "Your heart rate is a little high, but that's not surprising considering what you're about to do."

"I'm petrified."

"Okay, time to go," Ray said, walking into the airlock. He put on a backpack and helped Sarah with hers.

The kids ran in and gave Sarah a hug, telling her to be careful.

"We'll be back by dark."

Ray, Tony, Sarah, and Artie stepped out of the ship.

"The bracelet just snugged itself on my wrist." Sarah held up her hand and examined the band.

"It knows you left the ship, and it's just making adjustments so that it doesn't fall off," Ray said.

Sarah pulled on the band, it reshaped and slipped off her wrist. She put it back on and it once again secured itself to her wrist. "This thing seems safe."

Artie led the way toward the east and the rising red dwarf sun. Sarah was behind Ray and Tony brought up the rear as they hiked toward the blue forest and the distant hills and mountain range.

"At least I don't hear that sound we heard earlier," Sarah said. "Did we ever figure out what that was?"

"Artie, were you able to find out what that sound was?" Ray said.

"Sorry, Ray, but since I am not one hundred percent operational and there is a jamming device in the area, I was unable to determine the cause."

"What kind of jamming device?" Tony said.

"I am not sure, Tony. My sensors detect a disruption that is causing interference."

"If that's the case, how were you able to discover the crystal?"

"Like I said earlier, Tony," Artie said, still walking ahead. "The crystal is part of the life support system and is always given priority."

They continued walking at a good clip through the blue forest of the major leafed bushes and tall black trunked trees. It was like a dream.

"We are at the halfway point," Artie said, stopping at a small stream. "Would you like to take a break?"

Ray stopped walking and began taking off his backpack. "That would be good, Artie."

Artie turned toward them and kept standing while everyone else took off their packs and sat on them.

Sarah watched the stream's water flow over stones and listened to its babble. No, it tinkled. The sounds seemed clearer than normal, the colors more vibrant, and the air sweeter. "It feels rather—odd around here."

"I feel it, too," Ray said.

Tony checked the laces on his black combat boots. "I don't feel odd."

"Things don't feel amplified to you?" Sarah said.

"Nope."

Ray leaned back against a tree trunk. "It's the safety band."

Tony looked at Sarah as he finished stuffing his pant legs into his boots. "I told you not to put it on."

"It's a safety mechanism," Ray said. "It's just making you a little more sensitive to the environment so that you avoid harm. I'm told it doesn't work for everyone, though. I guess you're one of the lucky ones."

"I'm not sure I like it."

"You'll get used to it," Ray said. "Why don't you call the others and let them know how we're doing."

Sarah was about to touch the bracelet when it beeped. "What was that? I didn't touch it."

"Wow, that thing likes you," Ray said. "Most people have to activate the bracelet manually. But for you, it seems to be able to sense your intentions. You can even speak to it if you like."

"You mean it reads my mind?"

"No, it can't know your thoughts, only sense them."

Sarah spoke to the bracelet. "Call Infinity One."

"Sarah, how's it going?" Clare's voice came through the band.

"Everything's fine, we're just taking a break."

"We can see you and Ray as blips on a map. Can you see us?"

"Ask the band to bring up a visual," Ray said.

Sarah did as Ray instructed and a holographic image displayed in the air above the bracelet. "I can actually see you guys inside the ship. This thing's amazing."

"Now that you can see us, we can physically see you. How's Tony?"

"I'm fine, babe."

"Maybe you should have one of those things on. I'd like to be able to track you."

"Not gonna happen."

"We should continue the mission," Artie said.

"Looks like the android wants us up and walking already. I'll check in with you later." The call disconnected.

Ray reached over and touched Sarah's hand while pointing more things out on the band. A tingling sensation ran up her arm, she jerked her hand away.

"What's wrong?"

"Nothing's wrong. I felt something like an electrical charge when you touched me."

"I felt it, too. I think my implant and your band reacted to each other. It's nothing to worry about."

Then the implant in Sarah's upper arm—that she thought had quit working—began to burn. She put her hand on the area. "I think that thing just activated my alien implant."

Tony stood up and put on his backpack. "That's not good. Now the aliens might be able to find us."

"I'd keep the band on," Ray said. "It might be able to block signals from the implant and prevent the aliens from tracking you."

In the distance, a hollow bellow was heard like that of a Viking's signal horn.

"Artie, what is that noise?" Ray said. "Have you been able to break through the jamming device yet?"

"I detect a village of people directly ahead."

"Where is the crystal in relation to the people?"

"The dilithium crystal is located beyond them."

"Let's go to the top of that hill." Tony gave a nod toward the highest point past the stream.

"Artie, guide us to a vantage point where we can get a better look at the people and the crystal's location," Ray said. "I want to see what we're heading into."

Artie led them up the slope to an overlook. Ray took binoculars from his rucksack and looked down over a valley toward a village of thatch-roofed houses, wagons, and smoke from a smoldering fire pit.

Ray lowered the binoculars. "I see buildings but no people. Artie, can you ID them?"

"They are indigenous people of the planet. The jamming device that is employed is primitive, yet useable. They utilize both primitive and sophisticated technologies, leading to the conclusion that these people have been visited in the past by advanced beings. The horn is likely a warning signal. The crystal lies in the black forest at the base of the mountain, past the rapidly flowing river."

"They probably saw the spaceship land, and the horn is warning them about us," Tony said. "Can we go around them?"

"We could try and talk to them," Sarah said. "Maybe they can help us get the crystal."

"What if the dilithium belongs to them," Tony said. "Then we'd have to steal it."

"I can lead you around the village," Artie said. "But we would need to cross the river, and it is turbulent and dangerous. There is a bridge, but it would require going through the village to reach it."

Tony rested a hand on the pistol at his hip. "We do have weapons if we need them."

"Are they hostile, Artie?" Ray said.

"Unknown. However, I do not detect highly evolved weaponry."

Ray looked at Sarah. "If we go through the village, I want you up front because you don't look threatening. Do you think you can do that?"

"I hope so."

"Artie, take us to the village and then let Sarah take the lead when it's reasonable."

"Yes, Ray."

FIFTEEN

When they reached the bottom of the hill, Artie stopped at the edge of the trees.

Sarah looked out over a small, harvested field and the village beyond. "I wonder if I should take out my wand."

"Keep it in your purse and raise your hands," Ray said. "Be totally non-threatening. We'll be walking a short distance behind you."

Sarah was about to walk when Ray stopped her. He moved close to her and brushed her hair, causing it to hang femininely over the shoulder. Then Ray kissed her; a soft kiss on the lips. Sarah was not sure what to think because that same tingling she had felt when he had touched her hand earlier rushed through her body. She would have to avoid his touch.

"Ray," Tony said. "We have work to do."

"I hope you didn't kiss me because you think it's the last time you'll see me alive, did you?"

"No, that wasn't my reason." Ray smiled.

Sarah studied his face and then turned around, raised her hands partway and began walking toward the village. Suddenly, the horn blasted, startling her, causing her to stop. About two dozen men—blue-skinned men dressed in colorful clothes—ran from the building, forming a line. Each had a bow and arrow pointed directly at her. She was not sure whether she should speak or not. Then a big man, grasping a spear, walked through the line and stood a few feet ahead of the warriors.

"We come in peace," Sarah said, feeling somewhat foolish for saying a line that has been said in a dozen science fiction movies, but she could not think of anything else to say.

"I am Dah, leader of the Gunth province. What is your business here?"

"My name is Sarah from the planet Earth. Our ship has crashed on your planet, and we're searching for fuel so that we can go home." Mentioning the crystal did not seem like a good idea, at least at that moment.

"You, behind the woman, approach her."

"What is he saying?" Tony said. "And how does Sarah know how to speak their language?"

"Shh," Ray said as they walked up and stood next to Sarah. "My name is Ray."

Tony looked at Ray, bewildered by his foreign language skills.

"Say your name," Ray said.

"I'm Tony."

"What did he say?"

"His name is Tony," Sarah said.

"That other one," Dah said. "Who is he?"

"He is an android, our companion," Sarah said, trying to keep her voice from quivering. "He will not harm you."

"What fuel do you seek?"

"We need a crystal," Sarah said.

Gasps were heard as bow strings tightened.

"What kind of crystal?"

"A dilithium crystal," Sarah said, hoping she was not about to be pierced by a poisoned dart.

Then an old hunched over man with a crooked cane broke through the line and began speaking with the leader. When the conversation ended, they turned toward Sarah.

Dah held the spear at his side. "We have no crystals on Allanna."

Sarah looked at Ray.

"If I may speak, sir," Ray said, hands still raised. "Our instruments tell us there is a crystal on the other side of the river, at the foot of that mountain."

The old man spoke, his voice high pitched and wavering. "That area is forbidden. The black forest is not to be entered."

"We will enter at our own risk," Ray said. "We only need to cross your bridge."

"If you go there, you will not come back."

"We will take our chances."

Dah spoke with the old man and then said, "You three can come through, but the android cannot come any closer."

Sarah talked quietly to Ray. "Does Artie have to come?"

"It'll be a lot easier if he does. But I could instruct him to cross the river away from the village and find us later."

Sarah looked back at Dah. "It is agreed. The android will retreat."

Dah motioned for the guards to lower their weapons and to move aside. "Please, follow me."

They lowered their hands while Artie turned around and walked back into the blue forest. They followed Dah into the village. The alien race of blue people was now coming out of their shacks to look at them. Children pointed and giggled.

"Why are they laughing?" Sarah said.

Dah's grin was wide, revealing disturbingly large canine teeth. "They think you are funny looking with skin that color."

Sarah was thinking it was the other way around. But she was not worried because the villagers seemed friendly. One woman even offered her a drink from a hard-shelled cup resembling a coconut. When she looked at the inky black liquid it contained, she politely refused. It was not that she did not appreciate the hospitality, but rather, for all she knew, the beverage could be poisonous to humans.

They passed a spent fire that must have recently been used to cook a meal because the air still smelled of something like a beef roast. Sarah felt like she had been thrust back in time to a medieval village of peasants.

When they reached the wooden bridge, Dah said, "We have given you safe passage through the village and over the bridge."

"What about coming back?" Sarah said.

The withered old man looked up at them with cloudy eyes, like cataracts from old age. "You won't come back. The land is cursed. Those who have made it back across the bridge are changed . . . damaged."

SIXTEEN

Ignoring the warning, the three bade farewell to the villagers and walked to the long, dilapidated wooden bridge. They stood at the approach, considering the condition of the aged structure. Not to mention the rough rapids below it.

"It doesn't look too safe," Sarah said.

Ray stepped onto the deck, testing the strength of the timber below his foot. "Walk where I walk, and you should be fine."

Tony walked behind them, being careful not to put his weight on the boards on which Sarah stood. "Sarah, how'd you know the villagers' language?"

"What are you talking about? They spoke English."

"No, they didn't. They spoke some weird mumbo jumbo."

Ray continued moving forward. "The band interpreted it. Sarah thought she was hearing and speaking English, while the villagers heard their native tongue."

"How did the band do it?" Sarah said.

"I'm only the test pilot." Ray glanced back at Tony. "Do you want a safety band now?"

"Nope."

When they reached the center of the bridge, Tony looked down at the rushing water below them as it violently pushed against boulders. Then he looked both up and down the river. "I don't see that robot of yours."

"He'll be around," Ray said.

As they got closer to the other side, the air turned sour.

"I wonder if the wind always blows west to east," Sarah said, wrinkling her nose. "Because if it reverses, well, I feel sorry for the villagers because it smells like a sewer plant."

They stepped off the bridge and looked back across the raging water.

"Where'd they all go?" Sarah said.

"They probably don't want to watch us get butchered," Tony said.

The air was thick and humid. The black forest through which they would have to travel was dark and foreboding.

Ray took an instrument from his backpack.

"What's that?" Tony said.

"It's a high-tech compass. It will help us at least head in the right direction. When Artie catches up with us, he'll lead us the rest of the way."

Sarah took the wand from her purse. "This place is spooky. It reminds me of the creepy forest that Dorothy had to go through in the Wizard of Oz. Hopefully, the trees don't start throwing apples at us."

"I think apples being flung at us are going to be the least of our worries," Tony said.

Ray began walking through an open area of black spiky weeds toward the black forest. The others were right behind him. "We have to keep moving if we want to get back to the ship by dark."

"It feels like it's already dark," Sarah said.

When they reached the edge of the forest, Ray stopped. "Sarah, see if you can contact Artie."

"Artie, where are you?"

There was no answer. Sarah repeated the question, but Artie did not respond.

"The interference seems stronger over here," Ray said, looking down at the compass. "The source of the jamming device is coming from this place, not the village."

"That's not surprising," Tony said.

"Get the flashlights from your packs and let's keep going," Ray said.

The minute they stepped into the forest, the vibrant sounds that Sarah heard on the other side of the river had muted. Sounds were deadened, and the vegetation looked as though it was decaying. Maybe that was the source of the rank odor. They walked for over an hour, maybe two, stopping when even the flashlights they carried had difficulty penetrating the blackness.

"It feels like we're walking through oil," Sarah said. "I'm going to call Clare."

As expected, the call did not go through.

"The sun must've set, but it seems too early." Tony looked at his watch. He tapped the crystal. "I think my watch quit working; it says it's midafternoon. Check that device of yours, Ray. Make sure it's working, and we haven't been going in circles."

"As far as I can tell, it's working. Let's set up camp here and continue in the morning. We can't be too far away from the crystal."

Tony took off his backpack. "I'll get a fire going."

"Don't wander off too far," Sarah said. "You never know what's out there."

"Believe me, I'll be on the lookout for wild animals."

Ray unzipped his pack and took out a carry bag. "We each have a small tent. I'll help you with yours if you like."

While Tony gathered wood for the fire, Sarah and Ray set up the tents. Before long, Tony had a fire blazing and enough wood stacked close by to get through the night.

"Shouldn't that tin can have caught up with us by now?" Tony said, sitting on a rock next to the bonfire.

Ray poked at the fire with a long stick. "He should have."

Tony watched orange sparks float upward on the fire warmed air and crackle. "Hopefully he didn't turn to rust crossing that river."

As they sat at the fireside, they could hear something moving around them; possibly curious animals seeing what's going on. Howls in the distance made it clear that things like wolves occupied Allanna. But considering the unusual look of the people on the planet, what the wolves looked like—if that was what they were—was anyone's guess.

"We shouldn't let the fire go out," Sarah said. "Maybe we should take turns staying awake."

"That's a good idea. You can have first watch, Sarah. I'll take the second watch at—" Tony tapped his watch. "At whatever time you come get me."

When Tony had gone inside his tent, Ray took a thin blanket from his pack, put it on Sarah's shoulders, and sat down next to her. "I'd say it was a little romantic if wasn't for the beasts roaming around."

Sarah smiled as she watched Ray blow air into the surrounding coldness, causing a small cloud.

"The air's cooling down. I can see my breath."

"You're shivering. Want to share my blanket?"

Ray moved close to Sarah, letting her drop half of the blanket over him. "Thanks."

Sarah felt guilty snuggling next to Ray, but his body was so warm. Why should she feel like she was doing something wrong? Logic said Jack was dead. Even if he were not injured from the moonquake and the collapsing rim, the oxygen in his suit would have run out by now. Not to mention the fact that she and Jack were not even a couple. Or were they? Sarah felt an unspoken loyalty to him, and she was sure he felt the same way toward her. Commitment, for better or worse.

Sarah and Ray sat quietly next to the fire, occasionally tossing a log on the flames to keep it burning and the prowling critters away.

When morning—or what seemed like morning—came, no one had gotten much, if any, sleep. But it did not matter because the adrenaline was surging through their veins as they anticipated getting the crystal and returning—running—back to Infinity One with the fuel.

Still unable to contact the ship or Artie, they set out. Before long they had cleared the black forest and were standing at the foot of a mountain. Jagged black rocks like coal stood before them.

Ray looked up from the compass. "It should be around here someplace."

"I don't see anything that looks like a crystal," Sarah said.

Ray began walking along the slope. "Based on the map I saw on the ship; the crystal could be in a cave. So, keep your eyes open for one."

They walked along the stony embankment. Then Tony pointed toward a dark area on the side of the mountain. "Over there. I think I see a cave."

Tony led the way to what was indeed an opening to a cave. Much to their relief—at least as far as visibility—a dim light emitted from deep inside.

Ray looked at the compass and then latched it to his belt. Then he held the M16, ready to engage any enemy they encounter. "This has to be it. Have your weapons ready because I have a feeling that something else is using the crystal for fuel."

SEVENTEEN

As the kids and dogs came inside the ship, Max stood up from the control desk and stretched. "What does that poodle got on its back?"

Georgie bent down to get a closer look, then he jumped back. "It's a big worm."

Willis looked at Miss Foo who was now sitting quietly on the floor. "It's a bloodsucker."

Max looked at Father who was working at the lab station. "Father, bring some gloves and tweezers over here, will ya? We have a little surgery to do to remove a leech."

"Oh my," Father said, bringing the supplies. "Was the dog in the water?"

"No," Georgie said. "No one was in the lake."

Father put on the gloves and gently grabbed the fat three-inch worm, but he could not pull it off.

"Wait a minute," Max said. He went to the lab station and returned with a bottle in his hand. "I'll pour this rubbing alcohol on it, that might loosen it up."

As Max poured the antiseptic on the worm, Father wiggled the bloodsucker until it detached. "Now what do I do with it? If I put it outside, it might find its way back to the dogs, or us."

"Kill it," Willis said. "Step on it."

"Put it in the bottle," Clare said, studying the slimy predator. "If it'll fit."

Father raised the now squirming worm. It slipped from the tweezers, fell to the floor, and scurried off in a shot before anyone could catch it.

"Where'd it go?" Clare said.

"Over here," Georgie said, pointing to a grille near the floor. "It went in there."

"How'd it fit through that?" Max said, kneeling to get a better look at the protective vent covering. "Anyone got tools to get this thing off?"

"What's all the commotion?" Professor Dillon said, now awakened from the nap he was taking in one of the launch chairs.

"A giant worm got in the vent system," Clare said.

The professor lowered the footrest. "How the hell did that happen?"

"Here, Max," Father said, handing him a flashlight and a spatula. "I don't know where the screwdrivers are, but maybe the tip of that can be used to turn the screws."

Max removed the grille and shined the light into the vent system. "It's long gone."

"Maybe it'll die since it's not in water," Clare said, as she donned gloves and began examining the dogs for any more leeches.

Max stood up; his knees cracked. "I'll have that cyborg track it down when it gets back. Or better yet, I'll have him fumigate the place."

"Now I'm freaking out," Clare said. "There's a renegade bloodsucker inside the spaceship. You kids, stay inside with the dogs for now. I don't want any more of those creepy crawlers making their way inside."

"I don't see any more of them on the dogs," Willis said.

"I didn't either," Clare said. "But you might want to check yourselves for leeches. If they're anything like the ones on Earth, they have a way of attaching themselves to you, and you don't even feel it. I mean, Miss Foo didn't even notice it hanging on her."

"Gross," Dawn said.

"Let me see that dog," the professor said. "And bring me a pair of gloves."

Willis picked up Miss Foo and sat her on the professor's lap. He adjusted his glasses and smoothed out the dog's hair, examining the bite area. He stood up and carried the pooch to the first aid area where he cleaned the wound and applied an antiseptic. "Keep an eye on Miss Foo, that leech could've transmitted a pathogen to her."

Distressed looked spread across the kids' faces.

"Don't worry," Clare said. "I'm sure Miss Foo will be all right."

EIGHTEEN

Still unable to contact either Infinity One or Artie, the three stood at the mouth of the cave.

"The jamming device is probably located inside," Ray said.

Sarah looked down at the pebbles in front of the entrance for any signs of disturbance. "I don't think anyone has been here in a while because I don't see any footprints."

"Let's hope you're right," Ray said. "because if my hunch is correct, we're about to steal the villagers—or someone's—generator."

They turned on their flashlights and walked into the cavern. The floor was smooth stone; the walls were rough cut. As they moved further inside, toward where the tunnel curved, the light grew brighter. A humming sound was now audible as they continued until the path was bright enough to put away their lights and focus on their weapons.

Ray held up a hand for them to halt. They listened. All they heard was the dull, monotonous tone of what sounded like machinery being powered.

Sarah followed Ray around the corner. The sight was impressive. Through the chamber's open door was a round amber crystal, elevated on a golden altar by four spokes. Its glow was mesmerizing, shooting a weak beam of light vertically up to the ceiling and down through the center of the stone table. The room itself resembled an Egyptian crypt with hieroglyphics on the walls and a single tomb.

"Is that the crystal we need?" Sarah said.

Ray studied it. "Looks like it."

"It seems to me like most of its juice has been drained," Tony said. "Will it even have enough power to get us back home?"

Sarah mumbled under her breath. "Home? Do we even have one anymore?"

They lowered their weapons and walked up to it. The beam shooting below it appeared to penetrate through a basin that once held water. Above, the beam shot up to what looked like a decorative flush ceiling light.

"Is it safe to touch?" Sarah said.

"Should be, but it isn't like we have a choice." Ray looked at Tony standing next to him. "This is going to be heavy, and since Artie hasn't found us yet, you'll need to help me carry it."

"No problem."

"If we take it, will it harm the villagers?" Sarah said. "I mean, do they depend on it for some reason? Maybe they need the jamming device that it's probably powering."

"I doubt they even know it's here." Ray slowly brought a hand to within inches of the crystal. Then he quickly touched it and pulled his hand back. "It doesn't seem to be hot or cold. I think it's okay to touch. Artie wouldn't have assigned it to us if it was dangerous."

Sarah looked back at the chamber door, relieved it was still open. Then she watched Ray put both of his hands next to the crystal, sigh, and then grab and lift it off the prongs. She saw his muscles tense as he pulled it toward him and walked away from the altar.

"That was easy."

No sooner had the words left Ray's lips when the ground began to shake, and a screeching sound came from the sarcophagus. Its lid was moving.

"Run!" Tony shouted.

Sarah was first out of the room with Ray right behind her with the fuel.

"Faster," Tony said, looking back as he kept a firm hold on the pistol.

"I'm going as fast as I can," Ray said.

Rocks began falling around them. Ray tripped on one, and the crystal flew from his hands and rolled away. Tony helped Ray stand and went for the crystal, still rolling. He picked it up and everyone ran out of the mouth of the cave in a billowing mass of dust.

They ran away from the cave, toward the black forest tree line. Soon the shaking stopped, and the dust began to settle.

Tony shifted the crystal in his hands. "It was booby trapped."

"It wasn't a very good booby trap because we escaped with the crystal," Ray said.

"Don't speak too loudly," Sarah said. "Just because we made it out doesn't mean there isn't something else that could happen."

"Let's get out of here," Tony said.

Ray took out the compass as they walked back into the black forest, tracing their way back the way they had come. Tony and Ray took turns carrying the crystal and using the compass while Sarah stayed alert for anything that might threaten them. They continued this routine for quite some time when Sarah stopped walking.

"Quiet, I hear something," Sarah said.

Ray and Tony stopped and listened. Coming from behind them was the sound of something running directly toward them. Moving fast and hard.

"Run for it!" Tony said, carrying the crystal to the far lit edge of the black forest as though he was running for a touchdown.

Ray was ready to use the M16 as they broke through the trees and into the pasture. When they reached the bridge, Tony could go no further. Ray handed Tony the rifle and picked up the crystal that Tony had sat on the ground. The three of them were exhausted. They turned, only for a moment, trying to see what was coming after them. Tony raised the M16 as Sarah pointed the wand at the thing about to break through the trees.

"There it is," Tony said, ready to fire.

"It's a mummy," Sarah said.

"Looks like it can't go any farther than the trees," Tony said. "It's just standing there looking at us."

Then the village horn blasted.

"Let's get across the bridge," Ray said.

They cautiously tread across the rickety bridge. Ray's foot broke through a rotted plank, almost causing him to drop the crystal into the water. As they made their way to the opposite shoreline, they saw Dah and his warriors blocking their path.

Dah angrily pounded the butt of his spear into the ground. "What have you done?"

Ray stopped walking and looked at Sarah. "You tell them."

Sarah walked up next to Ray and pointed at the crystal. "We have gotten the fuel we need and can now leave your planet."

"No," Dah said. "The crystal must go back."

"Why?"

"I don't know what you guys are talking about," Tony said. "But that mummy is walking toward us. I think it figured out it can go farther than the tree line."

"That which you hold belongs to the Protectors, not to you. I did not know that was the fuel you were seeking. Now you have brought ruin upon my village and my people."

Sarah looked at Ray.

Ray's jaw tightened. "I'm not giving it back."

Sarah watched villagers run into their huts. She turned around and saw that the mummy was almost at the bridge. Then she looked back at Dah. "We can't take it back. There was a quake, and the cave was destroyed."

Sarah jumped when Tony began shouting at the mummy, telling it to not go any farther. She turned around and saw that it was now walking on the bridge. Tony fired a shot, but it had little effect. When she looked back at Dah, the guards had their bows raised.

"Give it back, or I will order my men to kill you," Dah said.

Behind them was the mummy, wrapped with filthy linen strips, and closing in. Before them were sharp tipped arrows taking aim. They were going to die one way or another.

Sarah raised the golden wand. She would have to use it, but who would she shoot first? The mummy. She turned around saw that the mummy was now halfway across the bridge. She told Tony to step aside, then she extended her arm, aiming at the mummy, but nothing happened. She tried again. Still nothing.

"It's not working," Tony said. He fired the M16 until the ammunition was gone. Then he took the pistol from its holster. "I don't want to use all our ammo. Let's get off this bridge."

Dah raised his spear. "Men, take aim."

Sarah turned the wand on the leader and his men. But again, it would not work.

Tony turned the pistol on Dah. "Let us through, or I'll put a bullet through your head."

Sarah was about to interpret Tony's demand when the movement to the left caught her attention. It was Artie running along the river toward them. "Look."

A few of the archers refocused on Artie and let the arrows fly. Artie was not phased and was at their side in seconds.

"Loose the arrows," Dah said.

Bows were drawn, and arrows were about to be released when Artie was in front of the men, grabbing the bows from their hands. He had caused such a ruckus that archers who managed to get a shot off missed everyone on the bridge.

Sarah, Ray, and Tony ran through the village as Artie tended to the mummy. When Sarah turned around, she saw the android and the mummy battling like wrestlers. When they reached the blue forest, Ray collapsed, he could not carry the crystal any longer. He let it drop to the forest floor. Tony sat down next to him and turned the M16 scope on the village.

"Who's winning?" Sarah said.

"The robot must've kicked everyone's butt because he's walking through the village toward us and I don't see the mummy anywhere."

Sarah brushed an iridescent beetle off a log and sat down. "So, Artie just saved our lives."

Tony lowered the rifle. "Don't get carried away. And why didn't your wand work?"

"I don't know."

"Probably that band had something to do with it. I told you not to wear it."

"Speaking of that," Sarah said. "Infinity One, can you hear me?"

"Loud and clear," Clare said. "What's been going on? We've been calling you."

"There's lots of interference over here, but we did manage to get the crystal."

Cheering was heard in the background. "Hurry up and get your asses back to the ship. I want to get off this rock."

"Is something wrong?"

"Ah, well, we'll talk about it when you get here. How's Tony?"

"I'm good, babe. We're on our way to you."

Artie walked up to them and stopped. "The threat has retreated, Ray. I suggest we begin walking."

"Thank you, Artie." Ray groaned as he stood up. "Your turn to carry that thing."

"Not my turn," Tony said. "GI Joe's turn. And by the way, Artie, where have you been? Get lost or something?"

Artie picked up the crystal with ease. "I seemed to have malfunctioned when I stepped into the river. I had difficulty repairing the fault."

"What kind of malfunction?" Rays said.

Artie began walking. "I'm sorry, Ray, but I do not know."

"That doesn't sound right," Tony said, handing Ray the M16. "Is there anything you do know about the malfunction?"

Artie continued to lead the others through the blue forest. "It is malware, and I am unable to remove it."

"Do you know the intention of the malware?" Ray said.

"Sorry, Ray. But it appears to have the ability to disable my safety mechanisms."

Tony looked at Sarah, then at Artie. "Does that mean the programming you have to not harm humans could be disabled?"

"It is a possibility, Tony."

"Don't worry," Ray said. "When we get back to the ship, Artie will be able to repair himself."

They pressed on, not stopping for a rest, anxious to get the crystal back to the ship before either the villagers or the mummy decided to come after them.

Infinity One was a welcome sight. Artie opened a door in the force field. They rushed through it, both weary and invigorated that they had accomplished the mission.

"They're back," Georgie shouted, running out of the airlock to greet them.

Artie wasted no time going into the ship and down to the lower engine deck to replace the spent crystal fuel. Ray went immediately to the flight console while Clare ran up and embraced Tony.

For a moment, Sarah expected Jack to be there to greet her, then, like a dagger through the heart she remembered he was gone. She collapsed into one of the flight chairs and watched the crew run around with youthful exuberance, knowing the ship had fuel and they could leave. But what was the point of leaving? There was no place to go, other than back to the moon to retrieve Jack's dead body.

Clare came up and sat next to Sarah. "How did things go, finding the crystal?"

"It was rough, but we made it," Sarah said. "It was inside a mountain cave in a room that looked like it was designed by ancient Egyptians. It had hieroglyphics on the wall and all that stuff. The really weird part was when a mummy came out of a tomb and chased us. But for some strange reason, my wand wouldn't work."

"When you're rested, let's go outside and test it."

"I'm rested good enough right now. I want to get this thing working again."

Clare stood up. "Hey, Ray. Sarah's going to test the wand. Can you open a door in the shield for us?"

Ray looked back at Sarah who was easing herself up from the chair, little by little. "I'll open a door straight out from the ramp, but don't stay out there too long. We made a lot of . . . people and things unhappy when we took the crystal."

"We won't," Clare said. "I just want to make sure we have a working weapon. I don't want us to get caught with our pants down if we're attacked."

"That's a thought, babe," Tony said.

Sarah and Clare walked out of the ship and to the rippled opening in the force field.

Sarah held up the wand and pointed it at a distant tree. "You know I don't really know how this thing works because somehow it just reads my thoughts."

"I know. Give it a shot."

Sarah tried, but the wand was lifeless in her hand. "It's still not working."

Clare looked at the band still on Sarah's wrist. "Now that you're safely back to the ship, maybe you should take that bracelet off. Maybe that's what's preventing it from working."

"Yeah, you're probably right." Sarah put the wand back into her purse as she struggled to take the band off. Finally, it slipped off, leaving a drop of blood on her red skin.

Clare gasped. "It was literally attached to you. Let me see it."

"Here."

Clare turned it so that she could see the side that had rested against the skin. "It's hard to tell, but it must have punctured your skin with a needle or something. It shouldn't need to do that if it's just reading your heart rate and blood pressure and is used as a walkie-talkie. It must be doing something else. Did you feel it?"

"No," Sarah said, taking an overused tissue from her purse to wipe the blood. "It felt fine. I had no idea. But that could be how I was able to communicate with the villagers we ran into. Tony heard gibberish, but I heard English and spoke English, or so I thought."

"At least you were able to take it off. Try the wand again."

Sarah held up the wand, and a thin beam of light struck the tree trunk she was aiming at. "It works now, must've been the band keeping me from using the wand."

Clare handed the band back to Sarah. "I don't know about using this thing anymore."

"I'll keep it in my purse for now."

"How about throwing it away?"

Sarah shook her head. "I don't know. It might come in handy someday. After all, it did help us communicate, and you were able to track us."

Clare shrugged as they walked back inside the force field.

"Oh, by the way," Sarah said. "What was that thing you were going to tell me?"

Clare stopped walking. "It's probably nothing to worry about. But Miss Foo had a leech on her when she came inside the ship. When we took it off, it somehow slipped from the tweezers and made its way into the ship's vent system."

"Oh, my god. So, there's a bloodsucker running around inside."

"I'm hoping Artie can take care of it."

When they got back inside the ship, Artie was back on the pedestal, standing like a stone statue.

Sarah walked up to the others gathered around the primary flight control. "Is the ship able to takeoff?"

"We're getting close," Ray said. "But everything looks good."

"Did that prisoner band bite you?" Tony said, looking at the blood still oozing from Sarah's wrist.

Sarah pressed the tissue back on the wound. "I guess. But at least the wand works when I don't have the band on."

Tony rubbed the back of his neck. "So, unless we can find Jack's alien pistol, we only have two working weapons. The wand—at least when Sarah's not wearing the band—and this pistol with three rounds left."

"What about the M16?" Clare said.

"Used all the ammo getting the crystal, babe."

Max rubbed his scraggly beard. "So what exactly is our destination? I doubt the aliens are done terraforming Earth. Besides, the bastard aliens are claiming it for themselves. Maybe we're better off staying here."

"I think we should go back to the moon and look for Jack," Sarah said. "Until we find his body, he's still alive."

Silence fell on everyone.

Professor Dillon took his glasses off and rubbed his eyes. "We arrived at Proxima b through a wormhole. Are we going to be able to use it to find our way back?"

Ray swiveled the captain's chair around and smiled at Sarah before looking at the android. "How are repairs coming along, Artie?"

"The crystal has given us enough fuel to last several years here on Proxima b. If we transverse back to where we came from, most of the energy will be consumed. More dilithium crystals will need to be found if we plan to bridge areas of space. However, I am working on conserving energy in noncritical areas."

Ray put his hands behind his head. "So, what are we doing? Are we staying here where it's reasonably safe, or do we look for Jack and risk running out of fuel?"

Other than Ray, everyone wanted to go back and look for Jack.

"Looks like I lost the vote. As soon as Artie finishes repairs and recharging, we'll jump."

NINETEEN

Jack could not believe what he was seeing. A beautiful woman—as beautiful as an alien female could be—sat up. She had pale skin and long white hair. A beaded draped dress covered one shoulder and was cinched at the waist with a belt. Based on the way her eyelids were painted with a black line that extended to the side of the face, there was no doubt she was related to ancient Egyptians.

She looked at Jack and with a soft feminine voice, she said, "Did you summon me?"

Jack stared at her, unsure what to say. He watched as she stepped out of the sarcophagus and approached him; stirring an aroma of bitter almonds. "I, ah, my name's Jack."

"My name is Hetepheres, one of many from the royal line." She looked around. "Where is your army?"

"I don't have an army. I'm trapped here, and I need to find my friends." Jack assessed her response to his answer. Did he say the right thing? Unless a weapon was hidden underneath the thin white clothing she wore, she was unarmed.

"How were you able to enter the portal shelter?"

"I'm not sure. I guess I touched the right spot by the door."

"Are you an Earthling?"

"Yes, I'm from America."

Hetepheres looked confused. "America?"

Jack explained his situation and how he was trying to get back to Infinity One or at least back to Earth. He looked at the Stargate. "Is that a portal? Can you turn it on?"

"You are an intruder and not allowed to use the portal."

Jack was desperate. He was not going to die on the moon. "I need your help turning it on and dialing it so that I can leave. That's why I opened your . . . bed."

"I appreciate your plight, but it is forbidden for mere subjects to use the portal. I cannot help you."

"You want me to die?"

"If that must be, it must be."

Jack searched his mind for anything that could possibly help him. "But I was able to get in here. The pyramid let me in. It must not think I'm a mere subject."

She paused, then said, "The portal shelter is wrong. It is ancient. Earthlings are not allowed to use the portal. Has it let you use it?"

The answer, of course, was no. Jack did not even know how to use it.

"I regret I cannot help you, Jack." Hetepheres began walking back to the sarcophagus. "You must leave."

There was no way he was going to let her go back to sleep. He ran up to her. "At least turn it on so that I can go . . . somewhere. Otherwise, I cannot leave. There's no air on the moon, and I need air to breathe, not to mention food."

Hetepheres kept walking.

Jack grabbed her arm, stopping her. "Why can't Earthlings use the portal?"

She looked down at the grip Jack had on her. "Because Earthlings are violent, aggressive, and not to be trusted."

Jack was hoping she would say that. Even though he felt like a lowlife, he was going to use it to his advantage. "Let me put it to you this way, sweet thing. If you don't let me out of here, do you really trust that I won't do anything to harm you and the others? I might strangle you all, what would I have to lose? I am an Earthling after all."

Hetepheres tried to free her arm from Jack's firm hold. She struggled until it was clear that Jack was not letting go and that he was strong enough to do what he said . . . strangle her. "I will break the law so that you can leave."

"Thank you," Jack said, releasing her.

Hetepheres walked up to the pedestal, swiped a hand over the dial, and the Stargate came to life. "I will send you to the nearest active portal. Please, go now."

"Where's that?" Jack said as he walked up the ramp toward the watery face inside the ring.

"I am sending you to the Roman god of war."

Mars? Jack put on the helmet and sighed. "What the hell."

Jack walked through the wavering undulations of the event horizon, emerging on the other side. He shook off the feeling of pins and needles and looked around. The Stargate immediately powered off; he was not going back to the moon, even if he wanted to.

He was inside another chamber, much like the one he had just left but larger. A lot larger. There were more Egyptian symbols, hieroglyphics, statuary, even more coffins, similar to but not the same as the ones on the moon. Jack had the impression that he was inside the Great Pyramid of Giza. Had the woman sent him to Earth rather than Mars?

Jack removed his helmet and walked off the platform, down the steps, searching for a door, hoping he was not now trapped in this chamber and would have to summon yet another alien from their hibernation bed. If he had to do that, they would probably send him back to the moon; a vicious circle. At least she sent him some place with air.

He walked deeper into the room, mesmerized by relief sculptures carved into the walls and vibrantly colored paintings on stone panels. Jack felt like he was inside a National Geographic documentary. He looked up and noticed the light coming in through a shaft. Then one of the statues— larger than Jack was—caught his eye. He walked up to it.

"You've got to be kidding. This isn't Earth, it has to be Mars."

The statue, though dressed like ancient humans, had a head that was not one of a pharaoh or a jackal, but of a reptilian alien, like the ones he had seen near the corral of strange creatures on the Martian base. "I've got to get out of here."

He saw a partially opened slab door. He listened for voices or people running his way, but it was quiet. Maybe they did not know he was there. But Jack was not going to count on it. Surely an alarm would sound somewhere—probably in the base with Randy and his cronies—when the Stargate was used.

Jack walked into the stone corridor. When he found a way out, he would head for the cave they had stayed in the last time they were on the red planet. Dealing with ol' T. rex would be better than dealing with these characters, especially Randy. Right now, Randy would likely have no idea who came through the portal. But once the mutated prepper realized it was Jack who had come through the gate, he was sure he would be tortured or stuck in the corral to be sold. At the very least he would be jailed inside one of the black boxes.

He ran down the corridor until he heard the terrible voice of Randy.

"Quick, to the Stargate."

Shit. Jack saw a dark crevice in the wall where the passage transitioned in form. No sooner had he slipped between giant blocks of granite, then he saw and heard Randy talking to a meek looking Egyptian or Oriental man.

"How could someone possibly come through the Stargate? Only people of the upper echelon have the privilege of its use. I can't even use it. Have you seen an emperor pass your way?"

"No, Your Eminence. I have not seen anyone. Is it possible there was a malfunction, and it powered on and powered off on its own?"

"I doubt it. Nothing happens by accident. Keep your eyes open."

Jack brushed a sticky spiderweb from his face as he watched Randy follow the warriors toward the Stargate chamber. Your Eminence? Randy? What a joke. He kept his attention on the unassuming man, with hands clasped and head bowed, walk the opposite direction. Jack followed him until it was evident how to exit the pyramid, which was what he did.

When he got outside, he took off running. The spacesuit was awkward and a hindrance to run in, but if he took it off, then Randy would know that someone had come through the Stargate and they would hunt for him. The tree covered cliff near the waterfall was the best place to seek cover. So he took off running across the plain, past grazing brontosaurs, to the area he had plunged into on his last visit to the inside of Olympus Mons.

Finally, Jack reached the shelter of ginkgo and cycad trees. He fell into the ferns, gasping for air from the high carbon dioxide levels. He looked back to see if anyone had followed him. No one had.

Knowing he would not need the spacesuit, he began taking it off. Then he realized that all he had on under it was the long underwear. He would wear the suit to the cave and then take it off there.

Jack looked around. Oh, how the place brought back memories; especially of Sarah and the time she and Ray came searching for him. If the truth be told, he would have to admit to himself that he was falling in love with her. Now Jack would never see her or the boys again. It saddened him, but at least he was alive. As long as he was living, there was still hope.

Satisfied no one was coming after him, Jack took his time walking through the trees and ferns to where the cliff turned to a sloping hill. When he reached it, he climbed to the top until he was back where they previously encountered the tyrannosaur. The only creatures in sight were distant flying pterosaurs, but they were too far away to worry about.

Everything was the same. The flowing river and the waterfall where Jack and the boys almost lost their lives. The steep-sided hill with the cave. All unchanged. As far as he could tell, no one had taken up residence in the shelter.

When Jack reached the face of the rocky hill, he sat down the helmet and climbed up the boulders until he was standing at the mouth of the cave. He took off the spacesuit and, dressed only in the ventilated underwear and socks, he climbed down and returned with the helmet. He was safe. At least for the moment.

Memories of the gang sitting around the campfire telling tall tales would have to wait. Jack was thirsty and needed water. He picked up the metal drinking cup that was still where they had left it and went deeper into the cave. He wiped dirt from the mug and began filling it with water that was thankfully still dripping from the ceiling.

With a belly full of water, Jack walked back to the mouth of the cave and sat down. Now what? Was he going to have to steal pterodactyl eggs, catch fish, and set traps for prehistoric animals? He hoped not, that was not how he wanted to spend the rest of his life. He wanted back on Infinity One, that is if it was not buried underneath moon rocks. He did not think it was, though. Ray and the android had probably managed to fly them away from the moon. What a jackass. Ray had better not be coming on to Sarah. The thought made Jack even more determined to somehow—no matter how unlikely—find a way to get back to the others on the ship.

But now he was tired. Jack leaned back against the cave wall and fell asleep.

TWENTY

"Artie," Ray said. "Have you located that leech, yet?"

"Negative, Ray. Resources are being used to finish the repairs."

"Ray, ask him if he's fixed himself, yet," Tony said.

"Artie's removed the malware."

"Just make sure the malware hasn't tricked you into thinking everything's been eliminated."

"Ray, the ship is now able to create a wormhole."

"Thank you, Artie." Ray turned and looked at everyone. "Are you ready for another trip?"

"Is the ship programmed to go back to the moon?" Sarah said.

"I have put in the parameters for us to return down the same path that brought us here," Ray said. "But there's no guarantee we'll end up there."

Sarah looked at the professor sitting in the copilot seat. "Is that your conclusion, too?"

The professor shrugged. "As best as I can tell, but I'm not an expert in this area."

"Then I'm ready."

The kids came up the elevator with the dogs and got back into the flight seats.

"Everyone is secure, Ray," Artie said.

"Let's go back to the moon, Artie."

Sarah was more afraid this time than before, now that she knew what to expect. She would not watch her body and the chair become one; closed eyes would be the way to go.

Artie lifted Infinity One from the planet and put it into orbit. Then the countdown began. The engine fired and the ship shot through the wormhole. Sarah could not keep her eyes closed. She watched the colorful writhing of the serpentine tube through the forward window. Then, no sooner had the trip began, when it ended. The Earth and moon were before them, but only for a moment because they were pulled into a weak secondary wormhole which took them to Mars and planted Infinity One on a grassy plain before powering off.

"What the hell just happened?" Max said. "I saw the moon, and now it appears we're back inside Mars. We would've been better off staying on Proxima b rather than having to deal with Randy who I assume is still here."

"I don't know," Ray said. "Artie, why are we on Mars?"

"I am sorry, Ray, but the ship's security system detected the spacesuit that Jack was wearing. Infinity One is attempting to rescue Jack. I tried to override it but was unable."

"Override it?" Tony said. "Why would you override it? The whole point of going to the moon was to find Jack."

Artie did not answer.

"Ray, can you explain that?" Sarah said, unbuckling her safety belt.

Ray's attention was on the console. "No, I can't."

"Well, I for one am glad the ship had a mind of its own," Tony said. "Now we can rescue Jack."

Father walked up to the forward window and looked at the pyramids and the alien headed sphinx. "I want to know how Jack even got here."

"I don't know how that happened, but we are indeed back inside Olympus Mons near where we were before," Max said.

"The layout is almost the same as the pyramids of Giza," the professor said. "Except the sphinx has the head of . . ."

"A reptilian alien," Tony said.

"Engage the cloaking shield, Artie," Ray said.

"Cloaking shield engaged, Ray. I also regret to inform you that I have detected fragments of the malware still in my system. If I am unable to remove them, they may begin replicating. If that happens, you will need to delete and reinstall my programming."

"See, told ya," Tony said.

"Keep working on it, Artie," Ray said, ignoring Tony's comment.

"The base probably knows we landed," Tony said.

"I agree," Ray said. "The cloaking shield should keep us from being found."

"Doesn't the base have high tech alien instruments?" Max said.

"According to what I'm looking at on the screen, the base is rather primitive," Ray said.

"They'll still come looking for us," Tony said.

Max stood up and stretched. A grin spread across his face. "We must've just popped into the landscape because those magnificent apatosaurs don't seem to be disturbed by our presence."

Sarah walked up to Ray. "Jack's probably in the cave. Is the ship able to locate the suit?"

"Looks like you're right," Ray said, pointing to a pulsating light on the map panel.

"Let's go get him," Tony said, checking the pistol in his holster.

"I'm ready," Sarah said.

Ray stood up from the captain's chair. "I'll go, too. The rest of you need to stay on the ship."

"No argument from me," Max said. "As much as I'd like to investigate dinosaur land, I don't want to be captured."

"Don't forget the M16," Clare said.

"No ammo for it, babe," Tony said.

"I suggest putting the safety bands on," Ray said, looking at Sarah and Tony.

"The wand won't work if I have the band on," Sarah said. "But I do have it in my purse."

"You already know my answer," Tony said.

"Okay, as long as you have it with you." Ray looked at the strap of Sarah's crossbody purse cutting between her breasts and then looked at Artie. "Do we have enough fuel for another jump? We can't live here with all the hostiles."

"It is possible, Ray. However, I am having difficulty calculating. I will scan for more crystals."

Max sat back down at the control desk. "I'll help him. We're too close to that alien trading post, and I don't want to be sold."

"Who'd buy you?" Willis laughed.

"Very funny," Max said. He looked at Sarah, Ray, and Tony who were about to depart the ship. "Come back with Jack, will ya?"

"That's the plan," Sarah said, following Ray through the airlock.

Ray took a supplemental oxygen device from the wall and positioned it over an ear and the thin tubing under his nose. "This will make it easier to breathe."

Sarah did the same and walked outside into the humidity. A dragonfly, the size of a hawk, flew into a stand of palm-like cycad trees. "This wouldn't be so bad of a place to live if it weren't for the aliens."

Ray looked at the tracking device in his hand as he walked next to Sarah. "I agree, but since there are dangers here, I'd put that band on if I were you."

"She can't use the wand if she does," Tony said.

"You can take it off if you need to use the wand. I'm told it does lots of things that protects the wearer."

Sarah reached into her purse and took it out. "I suppose you're right, but it also gets under my skin, literally."

"It didn't hurt, did it?"

"No, I had no idea it happened."

Ray held out his hand. "May I see it?"

She handed it to him. Ray examined it and then held it near her hand, ready to slip it on. "It looks as it should. May I?"

Sarah slid her hand into the band. It immediately snugged against her skin. "Clare, can you hear me?"

Moments later Clare spoke. "I do, but did you put that thing back on again?"

"I'll take it off when I need to use the wand. It's fine."

"Keep in touch."

"This place is something else," Tony said. "I knew there was an alien base on Mars, but this . . . I never thought it looked like the Land of the Lost."

Ray looked up from the tracker. "The spacesuit is definitely in the cave. Let's go."

The three moved quickly toward the gently sloping portion of the cliff. When they reached the top, they ran across the savannah until they stood on the hillside below the cave. They shouted up, letting Jack know they were there, but there was no answer. So they climbed up the boulders until they stood at the cave's entrance.

Sarah pointed to the suit. "He was here."

"Maybe he's by the water." Ray used the handheld for light and walked deeper into the cavern and came back. "He's not here."

"He could be hunting for food," Tony said.

They stood at the mouth of the cave and looked across the river toward the hill on the other side.

"The alien base is on that hill over there," Sarah said to Tony. "But we can't see it from here; it's hidden by all those prehistoric trees."

"There's movement on the other side of the river," Tony said.

"Sarah, call the ship and see if they can detect what it is," Ray said.

"Clare, pick up."

"Hi, Sarah. What's up?"

"We see movement across the river, but we can't tell what it is. Are you able to make it out?"

"I don't know. I'll check."

"Artie," Ray said. "What is the movement near our location?"

"Hello, Ray. I detect apatosaurs eating ferns between Infinity One and the pyramid complex. I also detect three humans heading toward the pyramids. One is resisting."

"Can you tell if it's Jack?" Sarah said.

"Negative."

"It's probably him," Tony said. "Let's follow them."

"If they captured Jack, then they'll also find us," Ray said.

Sarah looked at Ray. "We're going after Jack."

The three dashed out of the cave, down the side of the hill and ran toward the ancient tree log still lying across the river. They carefully crossed the moist corky trunk, knowing that slipping and falling into the river would pull them to the waterfall.

"Which way did they go?" Sarah said.

"I think they went that way," Tony said, pointing toward the far edge of the forest nearest the direction of the pyramids.

They kept pushing on, occasionally pausing for short breaks and hoping the carnivorous tyrannosaur was not aware of their presence. When they reached the sloping plateau, they looked at the road leading from the forest to the pyramids in the basin.

"Three people just entered the largest pyramid," Sarah said. Then she held her wrist toward her mouth. "Clare."

"I'm here."

"They took Jack, at least I think it's Jack, into the largest pyramid. We're going over there."

"Artie," Ray said. "Can you track the people who just entered the pyramid?"

"It is difficult because there is interference inside the structure. However, I do detect another crystal inside the pyramid. I suggest retrieving it."

"Where inside the pyramid is the crystal?"

"Unclear at the moment, Ray. I will continue my attempts at breaking through the barrier."

Making sure no one else was coming or going on the dirt path, the three ran down into the valley and along the road until seeking cover behind the haunches of the sphinx.

"Don't forget that I only have three rounds left," Tony said. He looked at Sarah. "Take that band off so that you can use the wand."

Sarah pulled on the band, trying to remove it from her wrist but it would not budge. "I can't get it off."

"See," Tony said. "It's a prisoner band."

"It's not a prisoner band," Ray snapped. "If it won't come off there must be a good reason for it, like protecting you."

"I don't see how when it won't let her use the wand," Tony said. "It's protecting the human workers like Randy and whatever is inside the pyramid."

"So, what do we do?" Sarah said. "If nothing else, at least we can communicate with the ship."

"Artie, are you able to detect humans or aliens inside the pyramid, yet?"

"It is still unclear, Ray. However, the movement has gone deeper inside the pyramid."

"Since they're not by the door, let's go inside," Tony said. He looked at Sarah. "Keep trying to take that thing off so that you can use the wand."

Sarah nodded.

They ran to the pyramid and stood outside the door. There was a wall panel of symbols next to it. Ray pressed a few buttons, but the door would not open.

Sarah remembered how she could open doors on the alien spaceship. "Let me try."

She swiped her hand over the symbols and the door slid open with the heavy grating sound of stone against stone.

TWENTY-ONE

The kids were on the lower deck tossing a knotted towel around for the dogs to play with. One crazy throw landed outside Ray's cabin door. When Jibber ran to fetch the throw toy she stopped, and instead of snatching it began pawing at the door, wanting inside.

Willis walked up to the anxious dog who was now more interested in what was in the room. "Jibber wants in Ray's cabin. Maybe we should check it out."

"We shouldn't go inside Ray's room without his permission," Dawn said.

"But something's in there. Maybe it's the worm. Besides, Ray isn't here. He'll never know."

"Wait, before you open it," Georgie said. He took off to the recreation room and returned with three cue sticks and three pool balls.

Dawn took the stick and ball Georgie handed her. "What are these for?"

"Protection," Georgie said, handing Willis the weapons.

"Ready?" Willis said. He opened the door, both Jibber and Miss Foo shot inside.

"There's the vent," Willis said, pointing to the upper wall, near the ceiling.

"Is the bloodsucker in there?" Georgie said.

"I don't know, I need something to stand on."

Georgie helped Willis slide the desk next to the wall near the vent.

Willis climbed on top and looked at the grate. "I need a screwdriver and a flashlight. Check his drawers."

Georgie and Dawn began going through the desk and dresser drawers.

"Here's a Swiss Army knife," Georgie said, handing it to Willis.

Willis turned the screws until they came out, then he wiggled the grate until it popped off. Then to their horror, the leech dropped onto the desktop. Before it could be caught, or clubbed to death, it crawled underneath Ray's bed.

"Quick, close the door so it can't escape," Willis said, climbing off the desk.

The dogs were barking as Willis grabbed an end of the bed. "I'm moving the bed so be ready to stab it."

Willis moved the bed as Jibber jumped on top, causing the mattress to slip off the bedframe. The bloodsucking parasite was trapped in the corner. Before Georgie could skewer it, Dawn picked up the worm with one of Ray's work gloves and dropped it in a drinking glass. Then she sat a book on the rim so that it could not escape.

"Good job, Dawn," Willis said, leaning over to examine the captured alien creature.

"Look." Dawn pointed toward Ray's bed, now in disarray.

"It's the alien gun," Willis said, reaching for it.

"Is it Jack's," Georgie said.

Willis flipped the gun side to side. "Looks like it."

"So, Ray lied," Dawn said, keeping a hand on top of the book.

Willis opened the cabin door. "We have to tell the others."

"What about the worm?" Dawn said.

"Roast it and eat it." Willis laughed as he walked out of Ray's room.

"That's gross," Dawn said, picking up the caged worm. "I'm taking this up to show mom and grandpa. They'll know what to do with it."

When they reached the flight deck, everyone was surprised to see the leech and the gun.

"Is that the worm that was on Miss Foo?" Clare said. "And the gun, is that Jack's? Where'd you find it?"

Max ran over and took the worm from dawn. He brought the glass close to his eyes. "You're not getting away this time."

"The gun was in Ray's room," Willis said. "Hidden under his mattress."

"What a frillin' liar," Clare said, taking the alien pistol from Willis.

"Now that we have the gun, we gotta go help Mom and Tony," Willis said.

"You're right," Father said. "I'll go. Any volunteers want to go with me?"

"I'll go," Clare said.

"Maybe you should stay here," the professor said, walking over to see what Max was doing with the leech. "I'm not feeling very well. I think my blood pressure is shooting up. Those journey's through the worm holes did not do my body any favors."

Max glanced at Father who was staring back at him with raised eyebrows and a smile. "Okay, okay, I'll go."

"Who wants the pistol?" Clare said, holding it up.

"I guess I'll take it," Max said. He looked at Father. "Considering you're a man of the cloth, God might do a better job at protecting you, than me."

Father winked at the kids. "I am known as a zombie fighter."

"These aren't zombies," Max said. Then he shot a worried look at Clare. "Can you show me how to use this again?"

"For Pete's sake," Clare said. "I should really go. No offense, but you two are no match against those people, or aliens, or whatever they are."

"Have them take Artie," Georgie said.

"I don't trust that damned thing," Max said. "It still has malware in its system."

"I agree," Father said. "Artie should stay here and repair itself."

"Artie," Clare said.

Artie did not answer.

Clare asked again. This time Artie responded.

"Yes, Clare."

"Are you able to accompany Max and Father to the pyramid so they can help rescue Jack?"

"I am still managing repairs, Clare."

"Can the repairs wait?"

"Leaving the repairs unfinished will cause a setback, Clare. And possibly jeopardize the crew."

"The crew is already in jeopardy. I command you to go along with Max and Father."

"I'm sorry, Clare. But I only take orders from Ray."

"Contact Ray, then. See if he'll let you go."

"Ray is inside the pyramid with the interference, Clare. Priority dictates that I repair the ship for escape. Otherwise, any rescues are futile."

Clare sighed. "I guess you guys are on your own."

When Clare finished refreshing Max on how to use the alien handgun, he tried stuffing it in the back waistband of the tight goth jeans. But it kept falling out whenever he moved.

"Here," Clare said, taking off the hip holster that once held her .44 Magnum revolver before the aliens took it.

Max put it on and placed the gun into the holster. It was not a perfect fit, but it worked better than his jeans.

"I hate to ask this," Clare said. "But are you two planning on wearing one of the wristbands so that I can talk to you?"

"Not me," Max said, adjusting the leather belt. "I don't want my head to explode."

"I'm with Max," Father said. "I'll trust in God."

"Okay, then. Good luck."

"Here, take this pool stick," Georgie said, handing it to Father.

Father took the stick and walked to the airlock with Max. He turned around when he heard Clare laughing. "What's so funny?"

"It's just that you two are quite the pair. A priest with a cue stick for a weapon and a scientist with a black goth T-shirt that has a picture of a skull and says life in death."

The kids laughed.

Max rested his hands on his thin hips, unintentionally highlighting his skinny arms. "Your husband helped pick out these damned clothes. When we rescue everyone, you won't be laughing anymore."

"Pray for us," Father said as they walked through the airlock rooms and out of the ship.

"Don't forget the oxygen," Clare shouted after them.

TWENTY-TWO

Ray led the way down the square stone passage until it connected with an ascending corridor. He stopped. "Which way?"

Sarah looked down the current passage that descended into darkness. "I say go up. The floor is beginning to get wet and slippery."

They walked up the box-shaped corridor until a lateral hallway merged with it.

"There's light that way," Sarah said. "Maybe we should check it out."

They walked until they reached a vast library where a flame burned in the center of the room. Shelves of papyrus scrolls, clay tablets, and bound books lined the marble walls, along with portraitures and busts. Statuaries of Greek gods like Zeus were depicted with reptilian aliens at their side, at war with what appeared to be the people of Earth.

"This place is twisted." Tony's voice echoed through the room.

"May I help you?" said a voice from behind.

They turned around, surprised to see a bare-chested, bald headed man with painted eyes. His soft looking slightly overweight body was dressed only in a white kilt that stretched to his knees.

"Don't come any closer," Tony said, pointing the pistol at the man.

"My name is Sesh. I am the keeper of the Hall of Records. What is your business here?"

"I don't understand you. Do you speak English?"

"I understand him," Sarah said. "We are searching for a friend; his name is Jack. Have you seen him?"

"Ah, I see," the scribe said. "Someone was recently brought here for the sacrifice."

"What do you mean, sacrifice?"

"To appease the gods, a sacrifice is needed so that their blood runs under the altar." Sesh shook his head. "While this man for which you search is not holy, his blood nevertheless will do."

Sarah thought she was going to faint. Jack was going to be sacrificed? Tony grabbed Sarah's arm, holding her up as the pyramid shook. It felt as though the tons of blocks above their heads would soon fall and crush them. Moments later it stopped.

"That was an earthquake," Tony said.

"The gods are angry, and we need to satisfy their requirements to stop the trembling," Sesh said, bowing his head.

"Where'd they take him?" Ray said.

The scribe looked up. "The man was taken to the high altar in the King's Chamber, past the Grand Gallery."

They pushed past the scribe and ran up the passage until they came to steeply slanted, narrow passage with a very tall ceiling. It housed no decorations, carvings, or murals. It was a soaring space that connected two passages.

"What is this place?" Tony said.

"I think this is the Grand Gallery," Sarah said.

Tony looked down the passage to what appeared to be a low-ceilinged room. "Any idea where this passage goes?"

"I think it's something like the Queen's Chamber," Sarah said. "But we need to go higher to the King's Chamber."

Near the top of the Grand Gallery were three pink granite monoliths, forming the door to the King's Chamber. They knelt behind the pillars so that they would not be seen.

"There's Jack," Tony whispered, pointing toward the altar.

Jack struggled against the ropes that tied his wrists and ankles.

"Look at the weird looking people singing in white robes," Sarah said. "Are those the preppers from The Community?"

"Sure looks like it," Tony said. "And that looks like Randy walking up to the altar in a black robe."

TWENTY-THREE

Max slowed his pace as they ran past a herd of sauropod dinosaurs. Their long necks—at least six times longer than a giraffe's—were outstretched and feeding on horsetail rushes. Max stopped and petted the small head of the closest brontosaur. "Oh, you beautiful beast."

"Max, what are you doing?" Father shouted.

"Coming."

When they reached the largest pyramid, they stood outside its open doorway.

Max took the alien pistol from the holster and looked around. "These pyramids are in better shape than the ones on Earth. The casing stones are mostly intact. But that alien head on the sphinx is disgusting, at least as far as I'm concerned."

They walked into the pyramid and followed the sound of singing. When they reached the Grand Gallery, they slowed their pace, stopping when they reached the upper chamber and could see inside.

"The fifth seal has been opened," Father whispered, peeking around a monolith at the activity inside the room.

"What do you mean?"

"That altar is intended for sacrificing animals and humans. The people, or whatever they are, in the white robes are holy, and their righteous blood and lives will be offered as a priestly sacrifice to God as the blood runs down under the altar."

"Look again, Father. I don't have the best eyes, but those are not righteous people, they're people from The Community. They've been transformed into insect-like things."

Father squinted. "You're right. This sacrifice is meant to be offered to their god, whoever it is, not ours. This whole thing is an abomination."

"You better start praying, Father, because that guy in the black robe holding up his hands is none other than that bastard Randy."

Then they heard a whisper. "Hey, guys, over here."

They looked and saw Tony motioning for them to join him behind a long granite block supporting a row of pillars.

"You found the alien handgun," Tony said. "Where was it?"

Max shot a glance at Ray who looked petrified. "Ask Ray."

Tony looked at Ray who appeared as though he was about to run away. "I'll deal with you later."

"I can explain."

"Focus, people," Sarah said. "We still have Jack to save."

They watched as Randy put on a mask resembling the head of a jackal. The singing ceased, and the gathered crowd silenced. Guards with spears stationed themselves around the altar.

With the acoustics of a concert hall, Randy's voice demanded authority as it roared through the chamber. "The gods are angry with us and shaking our home with great tremors. Soon the volcano will become active, and we will all be destroyed if we do not offer the blood and souls of saints to the almighty."

"Yep, Randy's still a jackass," Tony said.

Sarah nudged his arm. "Shh."

Randy stood behind the altar table and held up a book that looked like the Bible. "The Good Book says; I saw under the altar the souls of those who had been slain for the word of God and for the witness they had borne. O Sovereign Lord, holy and true, how long before thou wilt judge and avenge our blood on those who dwell upon the earth?"

Father shook his head. "This is a perverted ritual. It's unbearable to watch and listen to."

Randy looked at Jack. "Then they were each given a white robe and told to rest a litter longer until the number of their fellow servants and their brethren should be complete, who were to be killed as they had been. But this one, lying before me, gets no white robe. He is the devil. His sacrifice will satisfy the gods."

Sarah tried desperately to remove the band so that she could use the wand but it would not release its grip.

The crowd began cheering as Randy lifted a silver paten and a gold chalice.

Jack tried to break the bonds holding him to the table. "You're frillin' crazy in the head, Randy."

"You know, Jack. I asked the gods to send us a sign of what we should do to appease them. And lo and behold, you showed up."

"Go to hell."

Randy pointed toward Cecil and the Cartwrights. "My brethren, here, in shiny white robes were willing to sacrifice their lives for the greater good of The Community. But it is clear that the gods want Jack sacrificed in their place."

Tony grabbed the alien handgun from Max's trembling hands, replacing it with the pistol, and motioned for Sarah to follow him.

Randy raised a large dagger over Jack's body. "No, Jack, you are going to Hell. Your body will be cast into the pit of the volcano. But not before your beating heart and blood are preserved and offered to the gods."

"Don't listen to him," Jack said, turning to the frenzied crowd. "Randy's mind is warped from the vaccine that he and the other Community members took. He's not thinking right."

Randy placed one hand on Jack's chest, over his heart, while he tightened his grip on the sharp pointed knife. Then he began bringing it down toward Jack's skin as though he was about to perform intricate surgery. Slow. Painful. Elation.

TWENTY-FOUR

Sarah had the wand raised even though she knew it probably would not work, but Randy and his cronies did not know that. She and Tony pushed their way through the mass of people and stopped in front of the altar.

"Drop it, Randy," Tony said.

Randy reached up and took off the mask while not letting go of the dagger. "Well, well, well. Look who we have here. It appears that the little witch has brought a bodyguard to rescue you, Jack."

Tony had a two-handed grip on the handgun as he kept his arms extended. "I mean it. Drop the dagger to the floor and put your hands over your head or I'll shoot you where you stand. And believe me, I'd like nothing better than to see you drop."

The guards were about to charge them when Sarah said, "This wand will disintegrate you and a great quake will befall the planet. Your god will be outraged."

The guards stopped.

"Don't listen to her," Randy said, still holding the dagger next to Jack's side. "She's just trying to scare you."

"But she's a witch. She has the wand," one of the guards said. "Only Rausuca and his men have wands."

"That's right," Sarah said. "Rausuca gave me the wand."

Randy was beginning to look nervous; the guards believed Sarah. "She's lying,"

Tony aimed the gun at one of the guards. "You. Untie him."

The frightened guard began untying Jack.

"Don't do that, you fool," Randy said, fighting with the guard.

Tony fired a warning shot past Randy's shoulder and everyone in the temple scattered, including the guard that was releasing Jack. Everyone, except Randy who was now holding the dagger to Jack's chest, almost piercing the skin directly above the heart.

Randy was enraged as he glared at Tony. "I must finish the ritual."

Sarah could tell Randy believed he was doing the right thing. It was sad looking at his vaccine induced bulging eyes, but she would kill him to save Jack. She pointed the wand at The Community members in white robes who had backed away from the scene. When they saw the wand pointed at them, it was all the motivation they needed to clear the chamber. It was pure commotion as people fought to leave the temple by the only exit available.

"Shoot him," Jack said.

"Back away, Randy," Tony said, stepping closer.

Sarah turned back to the altar and noticed Randy's grip tightening on the dagger. He was getting ready to plunge it into

Jack's chest. Then a thin beam of light hit Randy. He dropped. Tony had shot him.

Sarah and Tony ran up to Jack.

"Are you okay?" Sarah said, leaning close to him.

"I'm fine. Just get me out of here."

Tony took the dagger, still clutched in Randy's hand, and used it to cut through the knotted ropes. Then he helped Jack off the table as gunshot rang out in the back of the chamber.

"What the hell is Max firing at?" Tony said, handing Jack the dagger. "Let's go."

They ran back through the now empty temple to where Max and Father were still crouched down in the hiding spot.

"What'd you fire at?" Tony said.

Max stood up on wobbly legs. "I didn't. Ray took the gun."

"There're only two shots left," Tony said. "Where'd he go?"

"I don't know."

"Is anyone hurt?" Sarah said.

Jack wiped the blood from his chest as he zipped up the cooling suit. "I'm fine. Despite the fact Tony never smoked Randy for almost cutting out my heart. He must have a soft spot for Randolph Watson and his budding insect sucking mouthpart thingy."

"Dream on," Tony said. "Let's get back to the ship."

They ran through the passages, pausing at the corridor leading to the Hall of Records. The squire was standing at the doorway with a thick piece of papyrus paper in one hand and a reed brush in the other. He nodded at them as if saying that the events would be recorded truthfully.

As they left the pyramid, people were running down the road toward the base.

"Look. I can see the ship. The cloaking shield is down." Sarah said, pointing toward Infinity One. "Ray is almost to it."

"Let's get him," Tony said, kicking up sand as he tore after Ray.

Jack and Tony were ahead of the others as they passed the feeding brontosaurs. When Ray reached the ship, he turned and shot aimlessly at them before getting on board and pulling in the ramp.

"He has one shot left," Tony said.

Then, as they approached Infinity One, it began rising.

"You've got to be kidding," Jack said, choking for air.

Tony removed his supplemental oxygen and handed it to Jack as Sarah and the others caught up to them.

Sarah touched the safety band. "Clare, what's going on up there?"

No one answered.

"He's trying to escape," Tony said, looking up at the hovering craft.

"The kids are onboard," Sarah said. "Clare, Ray, someone talk to me."

Still no answer.

"Artie, this is Sarah, what's going on? Bring Infinity One back down."

"Does Artie listen to you?" Jack said, breathing easier.

"I don't know, but I do have the band on. It has to count for something."

"Sarah, I'm sorry," Ray said.

Sarah was furious, but she would have to speak nicely to Ray to gain his confidence. Otherwise, he might leave Mars with the kids, and she would never see them again. "Ray, what's going on?"

Ray sounded like he was about to sob. "I messed up. I took Jack's gun because I . . . I love you, Sarah."

Sarah looked at Jack and Tony who were fuming. She felt pity for Ray. "Ray, if you land Infinity One we'll be able to talk about it. Alone."

"I can't do that. It's not going to work out."

"Please, Ray. People might be mad right now, but they'll get over it. We've all been under a lot of stress. Think about it. I won't let them do anything to you."

Tony's muscles flexed as he pointed toward the ship. "That bastard has the laser gun pointed directly at us."

Sarah was panicked. "Ray, please. I beg you. Set the ship down so that we can talk."

"If I can't have you, no one can."

"I'm wringing your neck," Jack said. "Set the ship down, now."

"Jack, that's not helping," Sarah said. "Artie, I command you to override Ray's orders. He is sick and is no longer fit for command."

They waited for what seemed like eons, then Artie said, "Sarah, I acknowledge your concern."

"Thank you, Artie. Please lower the ship so that we can come onboard."

"I am sorry, Sarah. I cannot do that. Ray is still in command."

"Take him out of command."

"I am sorry, Sarah. That is not possible."

"Artie, Ray is sick. Surely you see that."

"Ray is sick," Artie repeated.

"People who are sick cannot command ships."

"People who are sick cannot command ships," Artie repeated, again.

"I think you have the android confused," Max said. "Keep talking to it."

Sarah nodded. "Artie, I am in command now, and I order you to land Infinity One and let us inside."

"Must fire upon you," Artie said.

"No, no don't do that. I am the commander and you are to store the laser gun."

"Store the laser gun."

Max wiped beads of perspiration from his face. "If this keeps up, ol' Artie is going to begin smoking and short-circuiting."

Sarah's eyes widened. "Artie, you are programmed to not harm humans. Is that correct?"

"Not harm humans."

"Artie, you are programmed to destroy things that will hurt people."

"Destroy."

"Artie, you must destroy that which is about to destroy me."

"Destroy."

Then Ray came on. "Good try, Sarah. But Artie isn't capable of destroying himself. It's not in his programming."

Sarah knew she was getting through to Artie, no matter what Ray said. The machine was at least considering the action it must take. She looked at the others. "Now what?"

"Ray, lower that ship, and we'll fight like men," Jack said. "Not the coward's way."

"Jack, I'd like nothing better than to knock you out and stomp on your ugly face, but I'm not up to it today."

Max whispered. "What else does that band do?"

Sarah shrugged.

Max examined the band on Sarah's wrist. He adjusted his glasses and squinted his nose, along with his eyes. "It appears to have tendrils going through your skin. You must have some power over Artie."

Sarah's jaw dropped. "Tendrils? Plural? There was only one connection point before."

"I'm done talking," Ray said. "Kill 'em, Artie."

TWENTY-FIVE

"Artie, stop," Sarah commanded. "Ray is a threat to humans and needs to be subdued. You just received an order from him to kill humans. What does your programming tell you to do?"

"I must protect humans."

"Correct, Artie."

There was silence as they waited to be zapped and turned to dust.

"Artie, can you hear me?"

"The ship's setting down," Father said.

They watched as Infinity One landed and its ramp lowered. Jack and Tony were the first on board. They saw Ray restrained inside a tube of blue light.

"Good job, Artie," Sarah said. "Where are the others?"

"They are locked on the deck below, Sarah."

"Unlock it."

Tony shot down the ladder while Jack sauntered up to Ray jailed inside the blue force field. "I always wondered about you,

Ray. Never did think you were quite right in the head; especially with that chip in your hand."

"Ya know, Jack. I thought the same thing about you."

Jack watched Ray's eyes look to the side. When he turned around to see what Ray was looking at, Randy barreled toward him, tackling him to the floor.

"Shit, we forgot to lock the door," Max said, running behind the control desk.

Jack and Randy fought until they were back on their feet, facing each other with raised fists.

Jack spit blood onto the floor. "I thought you were dead."

Randy laughed. "You idiots had the gun on stun."

Sarah saw the pistol that Ray had taken lying on the control console. She grabbed it and aimed the barrel at Randy. "Get off the ship."

Randy glanced at her. A wide grin formed on his hideous face. "You won't shoot me."

"Maybe, but I see you still have the prisoner restraint on. When we take off, it'll look like you're escaping, at least to the people in the control room on the base. And I think you know what happens then. You'll be blown to pieces."

Randy's cocky attitude turned to concern.

"I don't know about Sarah," Jack said, now harboring Randy's arrogance. "But I don't feel like cleaning your blood and guts from the deck."

"Artie, prepare for takeoff," Sarah said.

"Yes, Sarah."

"Next time I'll get you, Jack. Count on it." Randy ran for the airlock.

"I'm looking forward to it." Jack laughed as Randy exited the ship. Then he rubbed his sore jaw as he turned his attention back to Ray.

"Looks like Randy got the better of you," Ray said.

"Sarah, tell the android to temporally let Ray out of the . . . whatever it's called that he's in."

"Why?"

"I have a score to settle with him."

Sarah stood speechless.

"Do it, Sarah," Ray said. "It'll be all right."

"You both are acting childish. I don't want any more fighting."

"I'd do it if I were you," Max said. "You know they're not going to be happy unless there's one more battle."

Sarah rolled her eyes. "Artie, release Ray."

"Yes, Sarah."

Artie lowered the shield. The minute Ray was free, Jack had slugged him so hard that he flew across the floor, landing unconscious near the lab bench holding the leech.

"A knockout," Father said.

"Let's get him to the medical bay," Sarah said.

They carted Ray's limp body down the elevator to an isolation room in sickbay, laying him on a biobed.

"Artie, is Ray going to be all right?" Sarah said.

"The blow to the head has likely caused a concussion. He will need to rest. I will monitor his condition, Sarah."

"See if there's a way to lock this room," Jack said.

"Artie, are you able to put up a force field wall," Sarah said.

"Yes, Sarah."

Seconds later a transparent blue wall covered the room.

"Artie, let me know if Ray needs anything when he wakes up."

"Don't go all soft on him," Jack said.

"He's not that bad of a guy. He's probably suffering from some type of space sickness. Maybe jumping through those wormholes did something to him. After all, we know the ship wasn't fully tested when we took it."

"He's an astronaut, he should be used to that stuff. Besides, he just tried to kill us. Don't let him out until we know he's safe to be around."

"It's the curse," Tony said. "That old man in the village said that anyone who makes it out of the black forest will return changed or damaged. Probably because he's an MIB."

"We don't know if he's one of those men in black . . . but he does have that chip in his hand." Jack said. "And he certainly hasn't been acting normal lately."

Sarah nodded in agreement. "Artie, monitor Ray's mental status and keep me informed. Also, keep him confined to the sickbay room until I say to release him."

"Sarah, I detect people rushing our way. I advise leaving the planet."

"Take us someplace safe, Artie." Sarah pretended to be haughty as she turned to Jack. "Looks like I'm the captain of Infinity One, now."

Jack bowed. "May I, a lowly servant, kiss the captain?"

Sarah smiled as she made Jack wait for her answer. "Yes, you may."

Jack planted a warm wet kiss—mixed with blood and sweat— onto Sarah's lips as everyone whooped and applauded with joy.

"Hey, everyone," Father said. "It's Christmas Eve. Let's praise God and celebrate the season."

Max frowned. "Aren't there still two more seals to be opened?"

Father nodded.

Max mumbled a cuss word and then said, "Ask the GI Joe if this ship has any whiskey. I'm in desperate need of a drink."

"Me too," Tony said, pulling Clare close to him. "We never even got the dilithium crystal from the pyramid."

"Artie," Sarah said, still in Jack's warm embrace. "We want a party with lots of food and drinks. And . . ."

"As you wish, Sarah. However, I did not catch the rest of your sentence."

"Find us a crystal someplace else. I don't feel like going back to Mars," Sarah said, as Jack continued kissing her passionately.

* * *

Thank you for reading!
ConnieMyres.com

READ ANOTHER BOOK IN THE SERIES

Signs (Seven Seals Redux, #6)

Close to perishing, the battered crew of Infinity One must risk their lives—and sacrifice one—to assure that human life continues on.

The crew of Infinity One must return to Earth to get a synthetic dilithium crystal from the Intercosmic Space Program's main base in Marinette, Wisconsin. Without the crystal to power their spaceship and the cloaking shield, they'll be an easy target for the Zeta aliens.

As if that wasn't enough, the sixth seal of the Book of Revelation is fulfilling its promise of stars falling from the sky and the sun becoming black as sackcloth.

It's a race against time. Can the downtrodden crew retrieve the crystal before calamity crushes them? Will they give up all hope because of the impossible odds against them? Who needs to be sacrificed to save the others? Find out in this sixth book of Seven Seals Redux.

ConnieMyres.com

ALSO BY CONNIE MYRES

STAND-ALONE BOOKS

Jezebel • My Name is Mr. Dibble • Ring • Haunting of Ender House • Rest Stop Terror • Solus • Who Killed Sweet Violet? • Lucifer's Island • Raven's Ridge

PACIE ROSE MYSTERIES

Slenderman • Hornet

RANCOR

Rancor: A Paranormal Psychological Thriller (Books 1 & 2) Sinister Attachments • Unrestrained

SEVEN SEALS REDUX

Seven Seals Redux: The Complete Apocalyptic Novel Series (Books 1-7) White Horse • Red Horse • Black Horse • Pale Horse • Tribulation • Signs • Trumpets

SUSPENSE STORIES

Suspense Stories #1: Raven's Ridge, Lucifer's Island, Sinister Attachments (Suspense Stories, #1)

THREE SISTERS' ODYSSEY (SERIAL)

Read Episodes as Connie Writes Them

WATCH FOR SPOOKY SHORTS

A collection of creepy short stories, A-Z.
Spooky Shorts A-G: A Collection of Creepy Short Stories

Apple Pie • Black-Eyed Kids • Creature • Dungeon • Electric • Fairy • Genie • House • Ice • Joker • Kiss • Lucid • Minion • Neighbor • Obelisk • Pattern • Quest • Rumor • Squatch • Time • Underworld • Visitor • Wolf • X-axis • Yellow • ZoZo.

* * *

The complete list can be found at ConnieMyres.com

ABOUT THE AUTHOR

CONNIE MYRES writes books and short stories in the horror, mystery, suspense, and science fiction genres. She is an author, developer, and registered nurse. Sometime in the future—whether by choice or by arm-twisting—she will join the digital nomad movement.

Born and raised in Michigan, she has been creating stories since childhood. Children she had babysat as a teenager loved to hear her mystery stories, especially since she carefully included all the children listening into the storyline, causing suspense for everyone.

Connie's website: https://www.ConnieMyres.com

FEATHER AND FERMION PUBLISHING
Founded in 2014, Feather and Fermion Publishing proudly publishes horror, mystery, suspense, thriller, science fiction and fantasy stories. Our imprints—Oort Cloud Books and White-Knuckle Books—publish original fiction with the mission to entertain readers.

Author Connie Myres owns Feather and Fermion Publishing.

CONNIE MYRES

VISIT CONNIE'S WEBSITE

Visit Connie's website and find her blog, books,, podcast, and where you can follow her on social media.

ConnieMyres.com